WEEKLY READER
Children's Book Club
Education Center • Columbus 16, Ohio

PRESENTS

WILDWING
by Phoebe Erickson

OTHER BOOKS BY PHOEBE ERICKSON

Double or Nothing
Daniel 'Coon
Black Penny
Animals of Small Pond
Cattail House
Slip, the Story of a Little Fox

WILDWING

Written and illustrated by

Phoebe Erickson

Harper & Brothers   Publishers,   New York

WILDWING

Library of Congress catalog card number: 59–8967
American Book-Stratford Press, Inc., New York

WEEKLY READER
Children's Book Club
Edition, 1960

*To the children
of the Wind River Indian Reservation
Wyoming*

CONTENTS

x

WILDWING

WILD HORSES

With sirens screaming the plane zoomed down, almost touching the heads of the terrified horses. Through the pass they came thundering—black and brown, tan and white, mottled and spotted, a band of wild horses.

The Arapahoe boy Bronze Feather lay on a flat rock above the canyon. He was watching a golden eagle as it flew south and hung almost motionless above an old corral built many years before by hunters of wild horses. The corral posts, driven into the sand and held together by stout wire cables, were still strong and firm. But there had been no wild horses in Small Canyon for many years, he knew.

Now, hearing the distant plane, the boy turned over on his back to watch for it. The hum faded and then suddenly grew louder. It was a strange shrill sound, like the fire engines he had heard in the towns. Still the pale blue sky remained empty.

Puzzled, Bronze Feather sat up.

Then the sound was all around him. The air and the rocks seemed to quiver. Stranger still, it was not coming from above, but from somewhere down in the canyon. He crawled toward the edge of the rock. The plane must be off its course, or in trouble. Maybe that was why its sirens were screaming. A towering butte blocked the view to the north, but in a moment he saw the silvery-winged plane. It was just below him, almost touching the canyon wall.

"It's falling!" he gasped.

But now the plane came up with a hideous screeching and began to bank and dip like a swallow.

Then he saw the horses. A wild stampeding band, with wide-open mouths and nostrils, panting and screaming, weaving and stumbling just ahead of the plane. Mares and yearlings and wobbly-legged colts—all leaping and plunging in clouds of dust, trying desperately to escape their tormentor.

Plane and horses swept past. Newborn colts, trying to keep up with their mothers, gave piteous cries as they stumbled along behind.

Bronze Feather stared down in bewilderment. Was the pilot doing this for fun—or was he in trouble and trying to bring his plane down? The boy watched to see if it would turn or climb higher, but when it kept diving into the dust that now concealed the horses he suddenly understood. His grandfather, Long Bow, had spoken of this new way of hunting wild horses. They were being driven toward the old corral, where wranglers would rope them.

He leaped to his feet. The wranglers would be following the plane, or maybe they were hiding among the buttes at the south end of the canyon. He made his way swiftly around rocks and through brush, slid down a steep grade, and knew he was in the grotto where he and his grandfather had once camped while deer hunting. Only after he had made the laborious climb up the opposite cliff did he remember that a narrow opening led from the grotto out to Small Canyon.

Up on the heights again, he found a deer trail, and when at last he looked down from the canyon rim, the corral was directly below. Milling around it were the horses, some trying to climb the steep shale slopes of the canyon, some standing with lowered heads and heaving flanks, getting a brief moment of rest while the plane soared over the mountains to the south. One group turned and wheeled in confusion around their leader, a huge buckskin stallion. But there was little comfort to be got from him, for though his head was still high, he too looked around for a way of escape. He too was cornered.

The plane came roaring back and circled above the corral as if in search of something. "He's looking for the wranglers," thought Bronze Feather, and wondered why they had not appeared. But, watching the terrified horses, the boy's black eyes narrowed under his sombrero.

"Away, evil one!" he shouted in Arapahoe, and shook his fist at the plane. This was one of the white man's ways of doing things, he thought. The easy way, destroying more than he had need for, the way he had destroyed the buffalo. The plane banked and dipped a few times and then turned northward, gleaming silver in the sun.

While the rest of his band waited, the buckskin stallion climbed to the top of the rocky ledge, where he stood with head flung high, sorting the scents on the air with wide-opened nostrils. Welts and scars on his clay-colored body were the record of battles with others of his kind. Fear and hate gleamed from his white-rolled eyes.

To Bronze Feather the stallion seemed enormous. Beautiful, but wild and unconquered. Such a horse as his grandfather would have captured and tamed in days gone by when men rode out on the plains and matched wits with the horses, taking them with skill and taming them with kindness. Long Bow told many stories of an Indian's love for his horse. The boy, remembering this, turned a grim face toward the north and waited for the wranglers to come. Now the stallion came down from the rock ledge and moved slowly up the canyon. His band followed obediently, taking snatches at whatever graze they could find. One gaunt black mare kept turning back to probe with her nose at a colt lying in the sand. It did not move, and at last she too followed.

Up on the canyon rim Bronze Feather moved northward with the horses, and, seeing them paw at the sand in a dry wash, he knew they were as thirsty as he was himself. It was his own thirst that finally sharpened his wits. There was a spring in the grotto, and a narrow pass led from it, going west, away from the canyon. Maybe he could help them find it—maybe they could escape!

The thought filled him with excitement; he began to run, circling away from the rim. The way to the grotto seemed endless, but at last he reached the edge of the cliff and saw the glint of water below. In a moment he had slid down the trunk of a tree and was at the bottom. Tall grass and flowering plants grew around the spring that welled up under a great hanging rock. But would the horses find the entrance from the canyon? Somehow that did not seem likely, for it was narrow and quite hidden by growth.

Bronze Feather knelt and drank from the spring, and splashed the water over his face. He cupped it in his hands and let it fall back—scooped it up in his sombrero and hurled it against the rock. The idea that had come to him seemed foolish, but still it was worth trying. Maybe the horses would *hear* the water, the way one heard a waterfall.

He filled his sombrero and, climbing to a niche in the rock high above the spring, he poured the water down. The sound was beautiful! Up and down he climbed, grinning with delight each time the water struck below. Sometimes he stopped to listen and to watch the entrance to the grotto, and when winds stirred the branches he waited for the sound to pass before emptying his sombrero. A squirrel's chatter and the high thin cry of a hawk disturbed him; each sound and movement was important now.

But as time went on, his feet moved more slowly on the climb up. Maybe his plan hadn't worked—the horses might have passed the entrance or the wranglers might have come and driven them back to the corral. Well, he would try it once more and then go out to the canyon. He had tipped the hat carefully and shaken the last few drops in a wide circle when he heard a faint sound—a CLICK, like the sound of hoofs on rock.

Bronze Feather knelt behind a bush, holding his breath.

At the entrance to the grotto, bushes swayed slightly and twigs snapped. Then a horse's head poked through a tangle of growth. It was the buckskin stallion.

But, scenting something besides water, the stallion was wary, looking this way and that, listening, with ears sharply pricked. Assured at last, he snorted and tossed his head. Down he came, watching his footing, sliding and stumbling and nimbly recovering.

He stalked to the water in a lordly fashion and began to drink. Another head poked through the thicket above, and then mares and yearlings came grunting and sliding down. Colts merely tumbled and picked themselves up at the bottom. Soon the space around the brook and spring was filled with dusty, lather-streaked bodies. Dozens of ears moved backward and forward, mares jostled yearlings while colts waited for a chance to nurse. Grass was snatched at, but after each mouthful, heads came up in the wary way of wild horses.

While the horses grazed and rested, Bronze Feather crouched behind the bushes—worrying. Now was their chance to escape. The wranglers might come any minute. Cruel or not, the horses had to be hurried on. He rose carefully to his feet and looked around. What he saw cheered him. The stallion was moving toward the pass that led away from Small Canyon, and at his whistled snort one of the mares raised her head.

"Now," thought Bronze Feather, and, leaping to his feet, he yelled, and whirled his sombrero down over the horses.

They moved in a wave through trees and brush, plunging and snorting, crowding and pushing, but following the stallion, and headed for the pass.

The boy listened until the last sound had faded. Without them the grotto seemed dim and lonely, a dark walled-in place. Had they really been there? Or was this a dream like some of the strange tales his grandfather told? He climbed down and found the trampled remains of his sombrero. It was hardly worth keeping, but after scrubbing it in the spring he jammed it on his head and climbed up toward the canyon, going the way the horses had come.

At the entrance he waited and listened. There was no sign of the wranglers, and no sound but the wind. There was no reason to hurry—the horses were gone, and even their tracks had been swept from the rocky ledge that skirted the grotto entrance. When he had scattered what little evidence there was of their passing, he ran down the slope. His moccasins swished the hot sand. It was good to be out in the bright sunlight again. And though it was still a long way to the trail that led up the cliffs to his home, it would be easy going in the canyon. It was not much past noon, for the buttes and the walls cast little shadow. He loped along, back to the wind.

WILDWING

Bronze Feather almost stumbled over the tiny colt. If it had not moved, struggling to rise, he would have passed it, for its color was that of the whirling sand. It shied away from his hand, its dark eyes rolling with true wild-horse spirit, its fuzzy ears lying flat in babyish anger. Its attempt at defense seemed so silly to Bronze Feather that he laughed aloud.

"I will not harm you, little one," he said in Arapahoe. Kneeling down, he reached toward it again, letting the colt snuffle his hand. Then he moved closer, and both arms encircled the small soft body. He felt it tremble, and held it closer.

12

They stayed so for a while together.

"You are alone and lost," he murmured at last. But even as he said it, Bronze Feather knew better. The mare was lying nearby in a clump of mesquite, lying too still for sleep. She had guarded her foal to the end, for there were signs of recent battle—broken twigs and deep hoofmarks in the sand.

"Coyotes," muttered the boy. Well, he had tricked them this time. A fierce joy came over him. This was surely the foal of the great buckskin stallion, but now it belonged to him. He had found it, and no one else could claim it—not even the wranglers if they should come.

He began to plan. He would tame it, and they would race together over the plains as free and as swift as the wild-winged eagle. Ha, he had named it—Wildwing!

"Wildwing, Wildwing, that is your name," he whispered.

Bronze Feather arose slowly with the colt in his arms. It was not as heavy as he had expected, but

its long dangling legs brushed the bushes. He lifted it higher under his arms, and, fearing that it would struggle at the sight and scent of its mother, he made a wide circle around the dead mare. Once clear of the bushes, he strode along, watching the canyon ahead and looking for places to hide in case the wranglers should come.

At first Wildwing seemed contented, but after a while his body began to quiver. Bronze Feather stopped and set him down on his long spindly legs. He took one step, swayed, and would have fallen except for the boy's guiding arms.

"You are not ready to walk yet, small silly one," he said tenderly. "First you must have milk to make you strong." He held out his fingers. Wildwing lipped at them eagerly, but, finding nothing, tossed his head in impatience. The colt was hungry, and the way was still long. Bronze Feather picked him up and went on.

Winds blew up puffs of dust along the floor of the canyon. The boy watched them appear and then vanish. Then far ahead he saw one that had a strange movement. He put the colt down and climbed to the top of a large boulder. The cloud of dust was coming forward against the wind, there was no doubt of that. But it was still a long way up the canyon. He scrambled down and carried the colt to the near wall, where a jumble of brush and rocks offered good cover. Wildwing sprawled out flat under a bush, and Bronze Feather, lying beside him, was glad of the chance to rest.

The three wranglers passed well below, riding fast, sombreros bent forward against the wind. They were mounted on good wiry horses, and the distance to the corral was not over a mile. They would soon be back, the boy thought; he would have waited for them to pass except that the colt needed milk. With luck he might make it to the next deep recess in the canyon wall before they returned.

He picked up the colt and hurried on. Sagebrush and mesquite tangled his feet and brushed the dangling hoofs. Shadows had begun to creep up the west walls of the canyon. His own odd bulky shadow lengthened under the hot sun. He rested a few times briefly, each time looking backward. But the whirling sand made it hard to see any distance, and now when he put Wildwing down, the colt lay quiet, making no attempt to get up.

A cold fear came over Bronze Feather. Maybe Wildwing had been too long without food—maybe he was dying. The boy stroked the mane that curled away from the small crested neck.

"We will soon be home—you will have warm milk," he whispered.

The distance between rests became shorter. His arms and back ached. He stumbled over stones and bushes. But each step counted, each one brought them closer to the trail that led up from the canyon. When he had passed the first hiding place, he set his eyes on a cave-like opening in the wall ahead. If he could make that—— A root snagged his foot. He was down on his knees in a sudden jolt. The shallow wash offered no cover,

17

so he eased the colt into a hollow in the sand and turned to look back.

At first the sand blinded him. Then he saw a horseman in the distance. Bronze Feather crouched down. His hands dug deep into the bank of sand above the sprawling colt. He pushed sand in layers over the small barrel of body and over the long legs. When he had finished, only Wildwing's head was visible, and that, lying flat and being the color of sand, would not be noticed, he hoped.

"Stay quiet, little one, I will be back." He sprang to his feet and hurried northward, shoulders hunched, head down. He had passed the cave in the canyon wall when a horseman pounded up beside him.

"Hey, kid. Seen any horses?"

Bronze Feather turned. "No horses in this canyon," he replied, and plodded on.

The wrangler galloped ahead and then, wheeling his horse, came trotting back. "Sure you didn't see any horses? We had a bunch of wildies in here somewheres. Rounded up this morning, an' they ain't come back this way."

"No horses in this canyon," repeated Bronze Feather without looking up.

A second rider came from across the canyon, and, reining in their horses, the two men kept pace with the boy. An argument started.

"Look, Sim, we'd have been here this morning if you'd showed up on time."

"Sure. Blame me. How'd I know the truck would break down?"

"Bah! We should've come out yesterday, like I wanted to. Then we'd been here when Van rounded 'em up."

"Something queer about this, Jake." Sim turned in his saddle. "I'd say we hit the wrong canyon, except there's some horse tracks around the corral. But where'd they get to?"

"Yeh," exclaimed Jake, "there's no way they could get out. We'd have met them if they'd come back. The kid here says there's no horses in this canyon, but we saw enough tracks to know different. At better than thirty bucks a head, we'd have made something on that bunch. Van said there was about twenty, not countin' the colts."

Sim pulled out his handkerchief and wiped the sand from his face. "Wonder why Clive ain't showed up. He's supposed to bring a dude from out east with him. Clive's after that big buckskin stallion hangs 'round in this Wind River Range. Shouldn't wonder if this wasn't his bunch of broomtails. Fastest horse in Wyoming, Clive says."

"I'd settle for one of that stallion's colts," growled Jake.

Bronze Feather's feet moved slower and slower. He longed to look back. The colt wouldn't move, he was certain, but still he had no intention of leaving him any farther behind. He began edging to the left, away from the riders. "I go up here," he called, waving his hand.

"Hey, wait!" shouted Sim.

"Oh, let him go," said Jake. "He's as dumb as a post. Keeps saying 'no horses in this canyon,' like a needle stuck on a record."

The third wrangler rode up, they spurred their horses, and soon all three were lost in a whirl of sand.

20

Bronze Feather raced back to the colt. Wind had shifted the sand so that he lay almost uncovered. But the trick had worked. Fresh hoofmarks passed only a few feet from Wildwing. He seemed revived by the rest, and raised his head at the boy's approach. Bronze Feather brushed the sand from the soft coat. "You were very brave, little one. But now we are on our way. The carrying tires you, but your own small feet would be too slow," he said, pressing his face into the silky mane.

With sunset the wind died down. The canyon lay in shadow except for the tops of the buttes and pinnacles. Catching the light, they were turned to deep purples and reds and were edged in brilliant oranges and yellows. Such a sunset was a good omen, Bronze Feather thought, and was reminded of the great buckskin stallion. This one, his own Wildwing, would be as strong and as beautiful someday.

It was almost dusk when he reached the trail that led up from the canyon. The way was not long now, but it would be harder with the steep climb.

21

His arms ached, and the colt too needed a rest from the constant carrying. They settled down on the grass behind some bushes.

Suddenly Wildwing raised his head. A queer little sound came from his throat. Bronze Feather sat up and closed one hand gently around the colt's muzzle. "Quiet, little one," he whispered, for now he too heard sounds coming down the trail.

Soon a rider and three lead horses swished past the bushes and turned northward up the canyon. The wranglers again. Would he never be rid of them? Now they were camped for the night and were watering their horses at the spring near the cabin. A faint smell of smoke came from their campfire.

Bronze Feather gathered the colt in his arms and made only one stop on the steep upward climb. A few stars were out when he reached the grove of pines that surrounded the cabin, but there was no light in the windows. Puzzled and rather uneasy, he put Wildwing down and listened for a moment. Then he gave one of the signals he and his sister had often used in play—the low *woo-hoo* of an owl. Still, all remained quiet. He moved closer and gave the call near an open window.

This time a soft *woo-hoo* came from the cabin. The door opened a crack and then swung wide. His twin sister, Little Bud, stood on the step.

"You were gone a long time," she said in Arapahoe. "Our father and mother have gone to Fort Washakie, and I was afraid when you did not come."

"Many things have happened," replied her brother. "But come and see what I have brought home."

Little Bud followed him to a clump of bushes. In the dusk she could see nothing but a white blur. "Oh, a wild goat! A fine white one. Where did you find it?"

"It is not a wild *goat!* You are very foolish. It is Wildwing, the newborn foal of a great buckskin stallion. Oh, I have a long tale to tell, but first we must feed him, for he has not nursed since morning."

"Will he drink cow's milk? There is some still warm from the evening's milking."

"Go bring it," replied Bronze Feather briefly.

Little Bud ran to the cabin and came back with a large bowl. They knelt beside the colt. Smelling the milk, he dipped his nose into it eagerly, spluttered and blew it in circles, but could make nothing of it.

"He has not learned to drink yet," said Little Bud. But with her fingers as a guide the colt soon tasted the milk and began to drink, his ears moving backward and forward.

Moonlight fringed the treetops and cast striped shadows among the pines. Coyotes barked somewhere in the canyon, and Bronze Feather knew they had found the dead mare. "We must keep this small one in the cabin tonight," he said. "Tomorrow I will make a place for him in a corner of the cow's corral."

They made a bed of deerskins beside Bronze Feather's low cot and the boy fell asleep that night with one hand resting on the soft wispy mane.

THE HIDING PLACE

Little Bud awakened very early the next morning. Tappings and patterings came from the kitchen below, and, remembering the colt, she smiled to herself. She dressed quickly and ran down the stairs. Bronze Feather was still asleep in his cot, but the colt was near the door, standing quite firmly on his long splayed-out legs. At first he was shy, but when she spoke to him softly in Arapahoe he seemed to listen and even reached out his nose for her to touch.

"You are up very early," she whispered. "You do not like to be in a house, I think."

When she opened the door he followed her out,

giving a little jump over the step. After shaking himself vigorously he lay down on the grass. The next minute he was up and on his way to the corral, where the cow eyed him curiously through the palings of the fence. Little Bud milked the cow and fed the colt from a small pan. Then he sprawled flat on the grass, and there she found him when she had taken the cow to the meadow.

She sat down beside him. How soft he was! And his color was almost like her new buckskin jacket. His legs and mane and tail were darker, she noticed, and there was a faint dark stripe along his back. He looked at her in wonder and then, with a sigh, closed his eyes and went to sleep.

But the sun was coming up over the far ridges and she had many things to do. "Up, sleepy head," she said in English. "You can sleep just as well in the corral."

The words sounded strange to her. The family seldom spoke English during the summertime when they came to live in their cabin. Her brother called English their winter language and Arapahoe their summer language. It was well to know both, their mother said. Ways of talking were funny, Little Bud thought. Their grandfather held stubbornly to their own language, but their father, Gray Wolf, would speak nothing but English.

Little Bud thought of this as she walked down toward the spring, swinging the two water jugs. It was not far, but the trail was steep. Early sunlight lay in flecks and stripes along the path. The day would be windy, for the tops of the pines rocked and sang in the way she loved. Gilias were in bloom, and here and there lupines held up their blue-flowered spears. The mourning dove called sadly, *coo-ah, coo-coo-coo*.

She was halfway to the spring when she heard voices coming from below and remembered what her brother had told her about the wranglers. She stood very quiet, listening.

"Horses—what horses!" a man was shouting. "We went all the way to the corral. Sand's covered their tracks, if there ever was any, which I doubt!"

"But Van said he drove a bunch down. The buckskin stallion was leading them. They *got* to be there someplace! Trouble is you fellows let them slip back past your camp last night."

"That's not so! And I can prove it. You didn't see any tracks goin' north, did you?"

"No, but we came through before sunup. Your outfit was still sleeping when you should have been up."

"Look, Clive. If you're so keen on that buckskin you go hunt him yourself. Count me out. This chasin' horses with planes don't suit me one bit. If I wasn't a paid hand I wouldn't be here."

Little Bud sat down on a rock to wait. These were the hunters Bronze Feather had outwitted, the men who chased horses with airplanes. Well, let them argue—they had got only what they deserved. But suddenly she sat up straight.

One of the men was saying: "What we need is a guide. Sim said there were some Indians living around here. *They* know this country. We don't. Your outfit can go back, for all I care. I'm going to find out what happened to that stallion."

" *'Some Indians living around here'*—that means us!" gasped Little Bud.

She raced back to the cabin. Bronze Feather was in the corral with the colt.

"The hunters are coming! I heard them talking down at the spring. They want a guide to help them find the wild horses!" she panted.

"Now? Are they coming right away?"

"I think so."

The boy picked the colt up in his arms. "We must hide Wildwing. Help me think of a place—quick!"

"The root cellar—where the milk is cooled?"

"No, no. It would be too cold and damp. In the cabin, somewhere."

They hurried to the cabin. Going through the doorway, Wildwing gave a squeaky little whinny.

"If they heard that, they would know," warned Little Bud.

Bronze Feather stood for a moment. "But that sound is also one of our signals," he said. "We can do it better than this little one, and without moving our lips. Do not worry, I have it all planned now."

Putting the colt down, he took a wide skirt that belonged to their mother from a peg on the wall.

"Put this on, and sit in that corner where the light is dim. You are mending it, but Wildwing will be under it. They are not likely to come into the cabin, but still we must be prepared."

Little Bud looked doubtful. "But how will I keep him quiet? See, even now he is in mischief."

Wildwing had his nose in a bowl of milk and corn bread which had been left on a bench near the door.

"He is hungry. Colts eat often and rest often," replied her brother. "Feed him again while I go out to listen. After that he will be quiet for a while."

The colt drank hungrily, and when Bronze Feather came back all was ready. Little Bud looked small sitting on the floor with the skirt billowing all around her. Under it, and quite lost in the folds of the cloth, lay Wildwing—sleepy again, and quite content.

"I forgot the needle and yarn," said Little Bud.

Her brother brought them. "The hunters will soon be here. I heard their horses. Remember, if the colt makes any sound, you must quickly make the same sound. I will take care of the rest."

Little Bud threaded her darning needle with dark blue yarn.

"I wish our mother were here," she murmured.

"We are not too young to be brave. Besides, there is nothing to fear. The hunters only want a guide, and I will try to keep them away from the cabin." He went out, closing the door carefully, and strolled a little way under the pines.

Soon two riders came up the trail. A saddled horse followed on a lead rope. They were not the wranglers Bronze Feather had talked to the day before. One was tall, lean, and deeply sun-bronzed and sat his horse like a man born to the saddle. The other one was fat and pink-faced. He looked like one of the many eastern tourists Bronze Feather had seen in the towns. And now, remembering that many of the tourists asked about wild horses, the boy wondered if this man was interested in them too. Cameras and field glasses hung from his shoulders like ornaments; his shiny new riding boots and fawn-colored pants looked tight and uncomfortable.

They stopped near Bronze Feather.

"Seen any horses in the canyon?" asked the tall man.

The boy raised his head. "Used to be horses there—many years ago. All gone now."

"Your folks home?"

"Not today."

The fat man took off his sombrero and wiped his face with his handkerchief. "Did you hear the plane that rounded the horses up yesterday?" he asked.

Bronze Feather nodded.

"What time was that? Morning or afternoon?" asked the tall one.

"About noon, I think," replied Bronze Feather.

"Hear that, Fred?" The tall man spoke angrily. "Van rounds them up at noon, and don't tell us till four hours later. No wonder they got away!"

"But I don't see how, Clive," exclaimed Fred. "The wranglers say they came right down, and if there aren't any passes leading out of the canyon——"

"We don't know that for sure," barked Clive. "This is new country for us." He turned in the saddle and faced Bronze Feather. "You the boy was down in the canyon yesterday?"

Bronze Feather stared up at the branches. "Yes. I was there. Small Canyon, we call it. A golden eagle has a nest there."

Clive went on. "Then you know about the old corral at the south end. Is there any pass down there where the horses could have gotten out?"

"Must be—if the horses are not there," replied the boy slowly.

"Real double talk." Fred grinned. "Let's get down to facts. Do you know this canyon? If you're a *real* Indian, you should!"

Stung, Bronze Feather replied without thinking. "I know it better than any white man. My people lived here a long time before *they* came."

"All right. Didn't mean to offend you. But listen. We'll pay you five bucks to guide us today. Fair enough?"

Bronze Feather hesitated. The horses were

gone, he knew; but, still, this would keep the hunters away from the cabin and the colt. Maybe it would be best to go with them. "O.K.," he said at last. "But no pay if we don't find the horses."

The men exchanged glances. "Oh-oh, something funny here," said Fred in a low voice. "I've read that Indians are great at stealing horses. Maybe they're hidden around here someplace."

"Sure. Look in the cabin. A bunch would fit in there just dandy," said Clive.

"I'll do that," replied Fred promptly, and began the laborious job of dismounting. "Always wanted to see the inside of an Indian house. Mind if I look?" he asked Bronze Feather.

"My sister is the only one home," said the boy.

But Fred had marched off ahead, and Bronze Feather ran to open the door. He stepped aside to let the visitor pass. Little Bud's dark head was bent over her work, the needle moving swiftly in and out of the cloth.

"How-do," said Fred. "Just wanted to look around."

Little Bud rumpled the skirt as if in search of the yarn.

"Kind of dark in here to be sewing, isn't it?" Fred's eyes searched the room. "You Indians make any fancy pottery or rugs?" he continued. "I like to get such stuff right from the Indians. The traders want too much money for it."

"Come on. Let's get going!" called Clive from outside.

But Fred had picked up a pair of moccasins. "What tribe do you belong to?"

"Arapahoe," said Bronze Feather, by this time quite worried.

"Never heard of them. But I'll give you two bucks for these moccasins. Bet that's more than the traders would pay you."

Little Bud shook her head. "Not for sale. They belong to our mother."

"How about the jacket? I'll give you a good price for that," said Fred.

"The jacket belongs to my sister," replied Bronze Feather.

Clive called again. "Come on, or I'll go without you!"

At that Fred stepped to the door. "Oh, no, you don't. I'm paying you fellows plenty to show me wild horses. Came all the way from New York to see them. Been reading about them all my life, and now when I get out here all I see is sand and rocks and a few miserable tracks. This cabin is interesting to me. I want to get a picture of the girl sewing."

Fred untangled the straps hanging from his shoulders and, after getting a flash bulb in place, squinted into his camera. "Now smile a big smile," he ordered.

Little Bud looked up at her brother. Just at that instant Wildwing sneezed, and the next instant Bronze Feather had made a perfect imitation of the queer little sound.

"What was that? Sounded like a horse!" exclaimed Fred.

"I did it. To make my sister laugh for the picture. Like this——" Bronze Feather made the

sound again. "I can do others." He gave a squeaky whinny. "My sister can do them too. Our grandfather taught us."

"Sure sounds real. Fooled me for a minute," said Fred.

"Here's an owl——" Bronze Feather hooted, and then barked like a coyote.

Fred kept taking pictures. "These kids ought to be on TV. They'd be a sensation," he said to Clive, who was watching from the doorway.

"And we ought to be on our horses," replied Clive.

When Fred had said good-by and gone out, Bronze Feather spoke to his sister in Arapahoe. "I will go with them now. It will keep them away from the cabin. But Wildwing must stay inside. Do not be afraid, I will not be away long."

Little Bud clutched at the skirt, which was heaving in billows around her. "Hurry. Do not wait to talk!" she exclaimed.

As Bronze Feather closed the door, Wildwing's head poked out.

LOST HORSES

Bronze Feather mounted the extra horse and they went down the trail. Despite a strong wind, it was hot in the canyon. The walls and buttes were flat gray under the intense light. A little distance ahead the three wranglers were waiting.

"Any sign of the horses, Sanders?" called Clive as they rode up to join them.

"Naw," replied the hawk-eyed old rider. "Sim was down to the corral before sunup, an' all he saw was a couple of dead colts an' a mare. If you ask me, we're wastin' our time!"

Clive spurred his horse, leaving Bronze Feather

40

and Fred behind with Sanders. Fred managed to edge his horse close to the wrangler. "What happened," he asked. "You say they found some colts and a mare—dead. How come?"

"How come?" retorted Sanders. "That's what always happens when you round up hosses with a plane. They go crazy with the siren, and run until they drop dead. The lousy thing routs them out of all their hiding places, so they never get a chance to rest. Should be a law against it, I say. Ain't hardly any wild hosses left any more."

"Sure sounds foolish," said Fred. "I don't know much about horses, and I didn't see the plane, but doesn't such hard running break their wind or something? How can they sell them if they're all worn out?"

Sanders turned to look at Fred. "You must be new out here. Guess they didn't tell you, but here's the deal. Those hosses are sold to fox ranches and to meat packers for dog and cat food. The shape they're in don't matter for that! See them big black birds up ahead? They're vultures. They an' the coyotes get the ones can't run no more."

They rode in silence for a while. High in the colorless sunlight the black birds hovered, dropping and soaring in circles over the same spot with a slight dipping motion of their wings. Watching them, Fred mopped his beet-red face with his handkerchief.

"That's awful—just awful," he kept muttering to himself.

Bronze Feather felt a certain kinship with the grizzled old rider, and wished that he could tell him what had *really* happened to the horses. This one would understand, he was sure.

Now they were passing the bare rocky ledge that led to the grotto, and he put his horse to a gallop to catch up with Clive. The spot seemed as solidly rockbound as any other part of the tall canyon walls, but still he was relieved when the whole group had moved past it.

The way narrowed and became a mass of huge jumbled boulders. They were nearing the south end of Small Canyon. Turret-like pinnacles joining the rugged walls formed deep recesses. In one of these the corral had been built. The stout cable-bound posts were still sturdy and strong, a mark of the past. All lay silent now; a desolate wind-blown place, without visible growth of any kind.

Fred and Sanders were the last to come up, Fred bouncing along in his saddle like a rubber ball. "No sign of life here," he puffed, reaching for his sodden handkerchief. His horse made a sudden movement, and, looking down, he saw a small shaggy-haired form half buried in the sand. The dead colt was a mottled tan and white, with a long stripe down its face.

"You see what I mean?" said Sanders.

"I see," muttered Fred, striving to keep his horse quiet and at the same time get his camera set. Despairing of that, he dismounted. His camera whirred faintly as he walked slowly around the colt. Back on his horse, he lit a cigarette with hands that trembled slightly. "Out East, they'd arrest a man for running a horse to death," he said.

"East is East, and West is West, but not *all* the West," replied Sanders, and moved on to where Clive and the other riders were gathered around Bronze Feather.

"Queer where those critters went," Clive was saying. "You, Feather, you say you know this canyon. Is there any pass?"

Bronze Feather wheeled his horse suddenly and pointed toward the mountains to the south. "Look! Vultures up there!" he shouted. And, galloping ahead, he put his horse up a steep slope where its hoofs sank deep into the sandy shale. Furrows had been torn through the rubble, and here and there in sheltered places were the oval marks of hoofs.

The other riders followed. At the top of the first steep rise they rested their panting horses. "You been here before? Know where this ends up?" asked Clive.

Bronze Feather hunched his shoulders. "Been all over—there's no pass here, but the vultures tell me something. Not far to go now, I think."

They began climbing again, and now the way was almost impassable. Upthrust rocks offered shelter to growth that tangled the horses' feet and tore at their flanks. They rested often, and at last reached a level place. The horse sign went to the left, over a sloping ledge. Here the going was easier, and though the way was narrow, it was not hard to follow in single file.

Rounding a towering boulder, Bronze Feather pulled his horse in suddenly and held up a hand. The others dismounted and came forward. "Don't go too close—might be a rockslide," the boy warned. He tossed the reins over his horse's head and slipped to the ground.

They stood on a rim that dropped dizzily into space.

Far below, vultures were circling above two large dark objects on a narrow ledge. They gazed in silence. Soon Bronze Feather turned away and went back to his horse.

"You think they *all* went over?" said Sim.

Clive shrugged his shoulders. "Could be. Who knows? That mutt of a pilot! He wouldn't have the sense to stop when he saw where they were headed. Horses go crazy from the siren, you know, and the thing drops off pretty steep here."

They stood around for a while, smoking cigarettes while their horses rested with heads down.

Nobody heard Fred's approach—nobody had missed him when he dropped back on the upward climb. Now he came up on foot, having left his horse a little distance behind.

"What's up?" he asked, seeing the men's sober faces.

"Oh, not much. Just a few dead horses," said Clive, turning away from the rock rim.

Fred looked down. He looked a long time, saying nothing. Then his camera began whirring as he moved slowly from side to side.

"That won't be much of a picture," said Jake, who was Sim's partner in the hunt.

"I think it will," replied Fred quietly. "As a matter of fact, I think it will make one of the best pictures I've ever taken." Then he turned on the men, his face livid with anger.

"I wondered about this way of hunting. Now I know. I'm an eastern tenderfoot, not supposed to know anything. But if I did a thing like this I wouldn't call myself a man. I'm ashamed to be here with you, and if I'd known your game you'd not had a cent of my money. Horse wranglers—baaah! You're horse killers!"

The men drew on their cigarettes and turned away, embarrassed at this outburst. But Fred went on. "As I see it, these wild horses belong to other people—not just to you! But with this way of torture they'll soon all be gone. The same as the buffalo."

"Aw, come on, we still got buffalo. They got their own range, protected by the government," said Jake.

"And if they didn't there wouldn't be one left," drawled Sanders. "I'm all for protecting wild horses the same way."

The argument went on while the men mounted and started back along the trail. Bronze Feather rode slowly behind them. Maybe a few horses had gone over the cliff, but not many—of that he was certain. And he had led the hunters to this place. Now they had seen for themselves, and had heard the wise words spoken by Fred and also by the old wrangler.

They went down slowly, the horses plunging and sometimes sliding. Fred was visibly shaken when they finally reached the flat floor of the canyon.

"Now you see why planes are handy for rounding up wildies," grinned Jake.

Fred straightened up in the saddle. "No, I don't," he puffed. "If riding were my business, I'd be in shape for it. And if I couldn't carry on my business without torturing animals, I'd get out of it."

"Well, you've a right to your opinion, and we've a right to ours. But we're in a hurry; want to get back to the truck before sundown."

Sim and Jake galloped ahead. Sanders waved his sombrero, and his black mare reared and then seemed to fly over the sand without touching it.

Bronze Feather rode behind Clive and Fred. "I'm glad now that I saw this hunt and got some pictures," Fred was saying.

"Oh, I'm not with that outfit," said Clive. "They're meat hunters. But Van knew I wanted the stallion, and this outfit was out after his bunch

49

of mares and yearlings. You wanted to see some wrangling, so I arranged it. The whole thing back-fired, but I'll see that you get your money back. No sense in your paying for any part of this trip. All you saw was a couple of dead horses."

As he listened, Bronze Feather became more and more uneasy. Still he kept silent. The thing was hopeless. These men would never understand why he hadn't told them at once about the horses, why he had agreed to guide them when he *knew* the horses were gone. They mistrusted him any-way—Fred's remark about Indians stealing horses, and his search of the cabin that morning proved it. No, it was better not to speak. This way they would leave Small Canyon—forever, the boy hoped.

When they reached the trail that led up from the canyon he dismounted quickly.

"Wait, Feather. You haven't been paid," said Fred, reaching for his billfold.

"No horses, no money. That was the deal," re-plied Bronze Feather.

"Don't be foolish. You earned it. Without you we'd never have known what happened to the horses."

The boy's dark face tightened. "I can't take money for that. We'll keep to the bargain." He turned and began walking rapidly up the trail. But he was being followed.

"Hey, wait," called Fred, riding up beside him. "Give this to your sister from me." He held out a five-dollar bill.

Bronze Feather stopped then and looked up. "What for?"

Fred smiled. "Oh, for being nice and posing for the pictures."

"She wouldn't want money for that!"

"Come on—take it," urged Fred. "She can buy her mother a new skirt with it; then she won't have to keep mending the old one. If you won't take it, I'll ride up and give it to her."

He was trapped now. There was nothing to do but accept the money or have them know about the colt. He crumpled the bill into his pocket, and managed a wan smile and a nod of thanks.

"Tell me," continued Fred, "you and your sister speak such good English. Do you go to school?"

The boy looked at him in surprise. This man seemed to have strange ideas about Indians. "Of course we go to school—in the wintertime, when we go back to our place near Fort Washakie. We all speak English, but we speak our own language too."

"Excuse me for asking," said Fred. "I've read about Indians, but you're the first one I've met. I guess I had the wrong idea about them; I think many people do."

"I guess so," replied Bronze Feather uncomfortably.

"Are you a full-blooded Indian?"

"Yes, sir." Bronze Feather's head came up proudly. "The Arapahoe were once a great tribe. Our grandfather tells us many stories about them. He says the white people could learn many things from the Indians, but our mother has taught us that we can learn from each other." He stopped, suddenly embarrassed at having spoken so freely before a stranger.

"I agree," replied Fred quickly. "You taught me something today—something I'll never forget." He leaned from the saddle and held out a soft hand. "Good-by, Feather. And stick to your ideas."

When Fred was gone, Bronze Feather walked slowly up the trail. He was thinking about his grandfather, Long Bow. The old chief would be pleased that the hunters had been outwitted. But that was the old way. Bronze Feather himself was troubled about it.

Through an opening in the trees he saw the black and white family pinto grazing in the meadow, and knew that his father and mother had come home.

A SICK COLT

Bronze Feather chipped at the weeds in the corn row, his hoe moving up and down with a faint clicking sound. The next row would bring him back near the cabin, and near the corral where Wildwing lay.

The colt was ailing, and at each turn of the corn rows the boy went to kneel beside him, to stroke the tiny face, to offer the bowl of milk and the fresh grass and certain healing herbs that their mother, Running Water, had gathered.

Wildwing was two weeks old, and at first he had seemed to thrive—drinking his milk, and frisking about in the yard, eager to play with anyone who came near. Bronze Feather had made a small cor-

54

ner in the cow's corral for his sleeping place, but the colt's wild heritage gave him a tendency to wander, and to show skill about hiding. He would be in full sight, and then suddenly disappear. Finding him was an exciting game for a while—he seemed to know his name, and would, if he felt like it, come when called. But mostly he would be found in the bushes, standing as tall as he could on his long, splayed-out legs, watchful and wary, a bit of his eye whites showing.

That was when Bronze Feather felt most akin to him and would put his face against the colt's silken mane and speak to him softly in Arapahoe. "We are alike, little one. For you are longing for something, as I am. You wish to be free, to go back to your own ways and your own kind. But if you stay with me we shall belong to each other— we will be strong together."

And so speaking, he would lead Wildwing back to the corral.

But one day, when Bronze Feather had gone hunting, Little Bud found the colt beside the trail that led to the spring. She almost missed him, for

he stood in a bank of wild flowers, a spot of dark gold among the tall blue spines of the lupine.

"Wildwing! Why have you come down here?" she exclaimed, worried because she had not kept better watch while her brother was gone. The colt came out at once and nudged the jug she was carrying. At the spring, his small nose bobbed into the water and came up dripping. As yet, his only interest in water was play. Little Bud dipped her jug and let it gurgle full.

"We must hurry; I have many things to do," she told him. And swinging the heavy jug to her shoulder, she led him slowly up the path.

That was the colt's last day of freedom. Bronze Feather, coming back from the hunt, saw the tiny hoofmarks at the spring, and questioned his sister. "Why did you take him so far?"

"I did not take him. He was halfway down when I saw him."

"Then you did not watch him, and that is worse. The coyotes or a panther might have gotten him," said her brother angrily.

"But I have other things to do. . . ."

Hearing the argument, their mother came to the cabin door. "Hush, do not quarrel," she said. "A wild foal is like a cricket in the grass, now here and now there. It is their nature to wander. But now that your father works for the white man at the ranch, there is much work to be done here. The foal must be kept in the corral, I think."

And there Wildwing spent his days, pawing at the poles of the fence, and neighing out his small soul in rebellion at captivity. Each call went through Bronze Feather's heart, and when he walked with the colt at evening, he noticed small cuts and swellings on the slender forelegs. He set to work smoothing the poles of the corral with his jackknife.

Little Bud was the first to discover the trouble. One morning Wildwing refused the warm milk she offered, and lay quiet, with closed eyes. "Wake up, little one," she said. "It is morning. Hear how the birds sing—they are not as lazy as you are."

The colt did not move. Little Bud, now rather

frightened, ran to waken her brother. They knelt beside Wildwing. For the first time they noticed the sharp outline of his ribs around the small barrel of his body, and the thinness of his neck.

Hearing their voices, Wildwing opened one dark eye, and one fuzzy ear flicked. Bronze Feather held the pan of milk close to the colt's nostrils. "Smell it, it is good. It will make you strong," he murmured. The colt showed no interest. There was nothing they could do.

That day Running Water and Little Bud worked alone in the cornfield. Bronze Feather would not leave the colt. He laid poles across the top of the shelter, and hung a blanket over them to keep out the sun. He offered water, and green grass, and plant tops; all were refused. He sat with the small head in his arms, saying any words that came into his mind.

"You must live, for you are the foal of the great stallion. He is strong and free." But his own words shamed him. *"Free,"* he muttered. *"Yes, maybe that is it . . . maybe that must be."*

59

He felt numb, letting the pain of this new thought flood over him. The corner of the corral empty—the dream gone—ended. It was his just punishment, of course. He had deceived the hunters, and even taken money. The memory of that still made his face burn.

He stayed with Wildwing most of the night, and though the colt drank some of the water, the boy knew there was little chance for a quick recovery, and maybe no chance at all.

He worked in the cornfield, coming back to the corral at each row end. But as the days passed, Wildwing lost his soft velvety look. He became a mere skeleton, homely, big-headed, and dull of eye. Only the strength of his wild blood kept him alive, for even the healing herbs Running Water had gathered worked no miracle. "The fever has him," she said. "He cannot live long now."

Bronze Feather checked his sudden unreasonable anger. "We do not know that. Perhaps he will be well in the morning," he said briefly.

That evening he walked the mile to the highway. Seeing nothing but the dreary stretch of rocky plateau, he turned south and climbed to the top of a small butte. Ridge after ridge cut into the clear evening sky. In the past, this had been wild-horse country, but now only the coyote and the panther and the deer shared it with lesser game.

The boy stood for a long time, watching the changing sky, his mind empty, his body weary. Here and there a star appeared, but there was no moon. He turned to go back, and then stopped.

A shrill screaming whistle ripped and tore at the darkness. It came once, and then again—savage, unearthly, echoing in waves of sound that ended in a whisper among the crags. It was not a cry of pain, or of anger, but a signal of freedom. To Bronze Feather it seemed joyous, wild, and challenging, like the sweep of a storm. Perhaps it was an omen, a sign that would tell him what to do. His grandfather believed in such omens, and he himself half believed. He went back to the highway and turned off onto the wagon trail that led to the cabin.

THE RETURN

Hearing her brother's footsteps, Little Bud ran to meet him.

"A strange thing has happened," she said excitedly. "I was with the colt, and he was lying with his head down as he does now. Suddenly there was a shrill loud cry. It came two times. You must have heard it; it was not the panther, I am sure. But *this is the strange thing*—Wildwing raised his head and tried to get up. He was much excited, and gave sharp cries in answer." She paused a moment and then went on. "He is not happy here. There is something he wants, I think, and that is why he is sick."

Bronze Feather's throat tightened. Tears came into his eyes. He blinked them back. Brother and sister walked slowly toward the corral.

"I too heard the cry," he said at last, "and now I know what it was. The band of wild horses has returned. It was the stallion who called. Wildwing must go back to join them. . . ."

"You would let him go?" asked Little Bud softly.

"He is dying . . . we cannot help him."

"But how can we take him back? He is not able to walk."

"We will carry him. I will make a litter with two poles and a skin stretched between them. He is not heavy now," replied Bronze Feather. "I will go to look for the band of horses before sunrise tomorrow."

They went to kneel beside the colt with hearts too heavy for speech, and when the boy would not leave, his sister brought a blanket from the cabin. He curled himself around the small wasted creature and slept with one arm thrown over the soft neck.

Long before dawn he crept out of the corral, and found a packet of food beside his gun just inside the cabin door.

Running Water did not question his absence, for Little Bud had told her of his decision, and she knew that his heart was grieved. The boy was in many ways like his grandfather, she thought as she prepared the morning meal.

Little Bud went out to the corral. Wildwing raised his head for a moment at her approach. But his eyes were dull and sunken. He drank some water, but turned away from the pan of milk she offered. Her eyes brimmed with tears. "Soon you will be happy, little one," she whispered.

The morning air was close and heavy. Thunder rumbled in the distance; dark tattered clouds moved swiftly over the mountains, and soon the tops of the pines were swaying. Little Bud hurried the cow into the corral, and as she ran to the cabin big raindrops spattered the dust in the yard. She burst in through the door, grabbed a deerskin from the floor, and flew back to the corral. By the time she had tucked it over the sick colt, rain was swirling through the trees in sheets of gray.

Running Water lighted the oil lamps in the cabin and added kindling to the fire in the fireplace. "It is good to hear rain on the roof again," she said, smiling. "The garden and the corn could not have waited much longer, but now we will have a good crop, I think."

"Yes, and it is the best time for rain to come— early in the morning," replied Little Bud, pulling off her wet jacket. It would be too wet to work in the field, she was thinking, and when it cleared she could help her brother with his plan.

Bronze Feather came back an hour later, dripping wet, but he had two good-sized grouse over his shoulder. With the steady soaking rain, and now more meat for the pot, their mother seemed unusually cheerful, and set about plucking the birds at once. Little Bud put her jacket over her shoulders and went out to milk the cow.

Bronze Feather followed her. "I found the horses. They were in the pass that goes westward from the grotto, and are drinking at the spring. I saw many tracks around it. They will stay in the pass, I think. There is still some grass in the grotto and many tall trees. The hunters in their planes cannot see them from above."

"Did you see the stallion?"

"No. I kept well out of sight so as not to alarm them. But I saw a strange thing. When I came back and was passing from the grotto entrance into the canyon, I saw a black mare."

"In the canyon?" asked Little Bud.

"Yes. But she was not grazing. She seemed to be looking for something."

"Her colt! Maybe she lost it when the plane ——" Little Bud stopped, staring at her brother.

They were sharing the same thought.

"She will *find* a colt," Bronze Feather said, and turned away.

By noon the rain had turned to a drizzle and the deerskin that had covered Wildwing was laced to the long slender poles with leather thongs. They lifted the colt carefully and placed him on the lit-

ter. Running Water walked with them as far as the spring, and then stood watching the sad little procession that went down along the trail.

The sun came out. Glistening drops fell from branches and grasses that brushed the sides of the litter. Wildwing was not heavy to carry, nor did he stir until they reached the canyon and stopped to rest in the shade of a tree. Then his head came up, and the dull sunken eyes showed a flicker of interest, as if some memory of the past had been revived.

It was cool in the canyon. Water tinkled and dripped from rocks and crevices. The walls and parapets glistened with dark wet colors, and above them, far to the east, a rainbow appeared. Seeing it, Bronze Feather felt the sadness in his heart lessen a little. A rainbow meant hope, it was a good omen—not for himself perhaps, but for the colt. He thought of the wild-horse hunters, and how he had tricked them. Maybe taking Wildwing back would make up for that.

They picked up the poles and went crunching

on through the rain-beaten sand. It was a long way. As they moved ahead, the colt became more alert and looked about with ears pricked forward and nostrils wide open. Each time they rested he squirmed on the litter, trying to get to his feet.

Their last rest was behind a huge boulder near the entrance to the grotto.

"Now we must be very quiet," Bronze Feather whispered. "We will leave him at the top of the rock ledge and then hide."

"But what if the mare does not come?"

"Then I will stay and guard him," replied her brother and slipping his gun from its shoulder strap, he leaned it against the boulder. He knelt down and held the colt's head in his arms. Words came, but for a while he could not say them. He looked up at Little Bud, and, reading the meaning in his eyes, she turned away.

"Wildwing . . ." he began haltingly. "You are free. . . . Grow strong and beautiful. . . . Do not be afraid. *They* will find you—and I will be watching."

He got up quickly.

Little Bud made her farewell in silence, letting her tears wet the colt's silken mane. They picked up the litter and went around the boulder.

Suddenly Little Bud stopped. "Look—look at Wildwing," she whispered. Her brother turned. The colt's head was up, his eyes alive and rolling. He gave a shrill whinny and tried to get up. Just then hoofs clattered on the rocks above. A black mare was coming toward them.

They lowered the litter and ran, for a wild horse might be dangerous, they knew. A bush-covered rock offered shelter. They scrambled to the top and lay flat among the grasses and leaves.

"It is the black mare—the one I saw," whispered Bronze Feather.

Below them, the mare began circling the colt, gradually coming closer. Her eyes rolled white, and now and then she gave a snort. Wildwing had tumbled into the sand, but now he was up—standing on weak wobbly legs, calling to the mare in high-pitched whinnies. He swayed and fell, and then struggled up again.

70

But the mare was wary, for the hated human scent was everywhere. On the colt, on the litter, on the wind. Her own foal had been lost in the flight before the plane; and though she did not know that, she remembered a loss—the small creature calling to her might well be her own.

She moved closer and closer, and at last her dark muzzle reached out to touch the colt's. They snuffed noses, making soft tender sounds. When his legs buckled and he sank back into the sand, she snuffled him carefully all over, her ears sometimes flying flat in anger, and again pricked forward. Satisfied at last, she nudged him, urging him to rise. In a moment he was at her side, nursing contentedly, his wisp of tail flicking back and forth.

Wind swayed the scattered harebells on the rock where Bronze Feather and Little Bud lay watching. Time passed, and still they lingered, for the thought of never seeing Wildwing again was not easy. The litter lay where it had fallen, and the black mare stood guard over the colt. He belonged to her now —they had no claim on him.

"I wonder if she knows he is not her own foal," murmured Little Bud, plucking at a grass stem.

"That we will never know," replied her brother.

But now the mare was acting strangely, flinging her head about, giving loud whistling snorts. A screeching neigh came from the rocks above. She began to prance, her eyes rolling, her mouth opened wide.

The intruder was an old tan and white mare, big-headed, clumsy, and rawboned. She advanced over the ledge with slow determined steps, and the black mare, trembling now with rage, began to paw the sand.

Little Bud clutched her brother's arm. "They will trample Wildwing!"

But the black mare was wise, and sprang out to meet her enemy. She flung herself up almost erect and with a wild cry came down on the old mare's shoulder. The old one staggered, and the black leaped again, this time sinking her teeth into her enemy's flank. With a scream of pain the old mare went off in a lumbering gallop.

72

The victor stood watching, but did not pursue. And when Wildwing came stumbling toward her she pulled him under the arch of her neck and held him close.

"We will name her Storm, for she went out to battle like a storm over the mountains," said Bronze Feather.

"HE REMEMBERS ME"

"It is good that you have found a wild mare to care for the foal," their mother said as she set bowls of corn and meat stew on the table. "But eat now, and be comforted. You have both worried for a long time."

"Thank you. We also are glad," replied Bronze Feather quietly. But he ate little of the food and soon went out to the cornfield.

The days passed. There was no talk of the colt. The fence that had made his small corner in the corral and the blanket that had sheltered him were removed. But each day, before sunset, the

75

boy took his rifle and disappeared down the trail
toward the canyon. He often brought back grouse
or a rabbit, but Little Bud knew that his way led
to the grotto and the pass that went westward.

Bronze Feather found no tracks around the
spring for several days, and began to wonder if
the stallion had moved his band again. Maybe
the human scent on Wildwing had warned him
of danger. Maybe the colt had been abandoned.
These and other dark thoughts came to him as he
walked through the dim silent grotto. On his way
out through the canyon he found the battered
remains of the litter. He plucked a wisp of sand-
colored hair that was caught among the thongs and
put it carefully under his sombrero band.

His loss seemed more real now—his last hope
ended. For until now he had thought that he
could somehow keep Wildwing near him. That
the colt was not really gone, but only *loaned* to the
black mare to care for until it was older and more
grown. That Wildwing could somehow know him,
and come back. But now that hope seemed ended.

Bronze Feather turned homeward, his feet dragging in the sand.

He did not go to the grotto again for several days. But one morning he awakened very early, and as he lay wondering whether it really was morning, the faint memory of his dream came back. In the dream he was leading Wildwing by a slender black thread. But the thread kept getting tangled among rocks and bushes. Then suddenly they were swimming a river, and the thread slipped from his fingers. That was when he awoke.

The patch of gray over his cot lightened gradually and took the shape of a window. Early morning! Why hadn't he thought of it before? Maybe that was the time the horses came to drink at the spring. He slipped out of bed and dressed hurriedly. By the time he had washed at the spring near the cabin and trotted down to the canyon, there were streaks of light in the east. It was good to be up early, to be running over the sand, feeling it spurt out from under his moccasins. Oh, he would find Wildwing—even if it meant going all the way through the pass to the high plateau country to the west.

He left the canyon before reaching the grotto entrance, slipping through the underbrush without snapping a twig. He had barely reached his old hiding place above the spring when he glimpsed the black mare among the trees. His heart gave a leap. A small sandy head was bobbing along behind her.

They were coming to the spring—they would be almost within reach! Bronze Feather hardly breathed.

The mare stopped, with a warning snort to the colt. Her head was up. She had scented something strange in the air. But now Wildwing was in full view. He seemed strong and nimble, and bigger than the boy remembered.

"You are Wildwing. You would know *me*," he thought tremulously.

He spoke to them, moving his lips without sound. "Storm, Wildwing, do not be afraid."

Storm snorted again. But the colt tossed his head and came on toward the spring, a miniature copy of the great stallion, proud and rebellious and, now, overly brave.

Even with his forelegs spread wide, his nose barely touched the water. His ears moved a few times in serious drinking and then he blew circles. Storm still lingered behind. The temptation to see if he was still remembered became too strong for the boy to resist. He grasped a root and pulled himself up to his knees. Then he crawled forward, inch by inch, until he was at the edge of the rock and just above the colt.

"Wildwing," he whispered softly.

The colt's muzzle came up, dripping. There was no fright in the dark luminous eyes but only wonderment. That voice, that whispering sound . . . The small head tilted upward. The eyes seemed to look straight into Bronze Feather's.

"It is me—remember me?"

They stared at each other. A long, long look—curiosity on one side, love on the other. Then the colt's tail flicked carelessly, and his nose sought the top of a tall weed.

Bronze Feather slid back under cover. He

wanted to shout. He wanted to dance. His fingers curled themselves around a root to keep himself anchored.

Storm came slowly up to join her nurseling at the spring. She was not at ease. The bony head came up often with ears erect and listening. Soon she and the colt wandered off toward the pass and were lost among the trees.

Bronze Feather rose to his feet. His knees were trembling. He felt light-headed and giddy. As he climbed the slope his eyes saw a large oval pad mark in the damp earth, but in his joy the footprint might have been that of a squirrel for all he cared.

"He remembers me," he whispered over and over.

Down in the canyon, he spread his arms and flapped them as if they were wings. He leaped high in the air and shouted. The distance back to the cabin and from there to the cornfield seemed as nothing. Little Bud, looking up from her hoeing, thought for a moment that their scarecrow had taken wing.

"I saw him! He was as close to me as you are! And he *remembers* me—he looked right into my eyes!" cried Bronze Feather.

Little Bud laughed and dropped her hoe. They capered about together, trampling corn and weeds alike.

THE PANTHER

After that, Bronze Feather went often to the grotto, always early in the morning. Once he caught a glimpse of the stallion, and guessed that he and his band had found another spring somewhere in the pass and only used this one if their grazing brought them near to it during the night.

In time the black mare, Storm, became accustomed to Bronze Feather's scent. Still, he was careful to keep out of her sight, and only whispered to the colt when she had wandered away. He watched her habits. She generally went back toward the pass after drinking, while Wildwing grazed here and there among the tall grass and plants. He seemed none too willing to follow her, or to heed her nickers of warning.

One morning Bronze Feather hid in the bottom of the grotto and waited for the pair to come. Just whispering to Wildwing was not enough; he longed to touch him, to run his fingers through the mane that now rose in a shaggy crest. "I must not let him forget me," he thought. "When he is old enough not to need the mare's milk I will take him back."

His plan was simple. It was June now; the colt was already beginning to graze, and had long ago learned to drink water. Before September, when the family would leave the cabin for the winter, he would bring Wildwing home and begin his training. Halter-broken, he could easily follow the wagon when they left. An extra stall in the small barn at their winter home would be easy to build, and the half-wild pinto might like company.

Bronze Feather's thoughts flew on. But suddenly he realized that the sun was climbing, and still the horses had not come. He rose to one knee, and then slowly to his feet. All was quiet except for a flock of magpies—unusually quiet, he thought. He looked toward the spring. His eyes blinked. That tawny spot—had that been there before? Could it be Wildwing? He watched for a moment and then took a careful step forward. The spot moved. *A panther was crouched over the water.*

The pad mark! He had forgotten all about it. But maybe Storm knew. Maybe that was why she had stayed away. His legs trembled. This time he had left his gun at home. *This very day,* when the big cat was within easy range of a bullet. Sweat poured over him; every nerve became tense with listening. The colt might wander away from Storm —might come ambling into the grotto alone.

Slowly, carefully, he reached down and picked up a small sharp-edged stone. He hurled it. The cat leaped, a tawny blur among the greens. The bushes above the spring swayed.

Bronze Feather waited for what seemed like hours. Was the panther waiting too? Did it know just when Wildwing would be within easy reach of its leap? He sat down on a log, sick with worry. One minute he decided to race back to get his gun, and the next, to stay and do whatever he could if trouble came.

At last he knew that it was useless to wait any longer. There was one comforting thought. Storm had been wise. She had kept Wildwing away. He felt humbly grateful to her. Once in the canyon, he moved at a steady trot. By noon he was on the trail that led up from the canyon, and he saw Little Bud at the spring with her water jugs.

"Where have you been?" she asked. "Our mother is worried. She does not understand your early morning wanderings."

Bronze Feather shook his head and, dropping beside the spring, drank in gulps and splashed water over his burning face. Somewhat calmed, he sat up. "A panther came to drink in the grotto, and by an evil chance I did not have my rifle," he replied.

"Was Wildwing there?"

"No. The mare did not come. But the colt is contrary. He might not follow her, for he was used to wandering alone when he was with us. I must get my gun and go back at once."

Little Bud looked worried. "First you must bring the pinto down here to water. He is too crafty for our mother or me to handle."

"The pinto! Where did he come from? Our father rode him to the ranch where he works."

"Our father is home. He is not well," replied Little Bud shortly.

There was no need for more explanation. With a month's pay in his pocket, Gray Wolf felt no need to continue a job he hated. It was the usual thing, and seemed right and proper to him, especially since he was careful to turn most of the money over to their mother. Jobs of this kind came and went, the ranches always needed extra help. Gray Wolf never worried.

"Oh . . ." Bronze Feather frowned. "Well, the pinto will not die of thirst before I get back."

"That is not the trouble. The pinto is sold. Our father traded him for a car, and he must be watered and brought out to the highway before Tall Man comes with the car."

"What?" shouted Bronze Feather, aghast.

"It is true." Little Bud picked up her jugs and walked ahead.

"Then our father is indeed not well. The highway is a mile away, and even our wagon can hardly pass over the trail. This is the most foolish thing he has ever done. But Tall Man would trick anyone," said her brother.

As they neared the cabin, Running Water came to meet them.

"You are back. And you got nothing—not even a hen?"

"I came to get my rifle," said Bronze Feather.

His mother stared at him in amazement. "Your rifle? Why would you go to hunt without it?"

"Because I am very foolish," replied the boy.

In the cabin, Gray Wolf was lying on the couch smoking. When Bronze Feather came in, he raised himself on his elbow.

"You're just in time," he said in English. "The pinto is tied in the meadow. Take him to water and then ride him to the highway. Tall Man should be there by now. He'll take the pinto. I've traded him for a fine car. A big convertible," he added with pride.

The boy stared at his father. "But we will have no horse—how will we move back when school begins, or plow our field next spring?"

"Speak English, boy. That's why you go to school," ordered Gray Wolf. "You have the colt. It will be strong enough to work by spring. Why have two horses? A car is better for travel."

Bronze Feather flushed in anger. His father's insistence on "speaking English" was part of it. But he obeyed. "The colt is gone," he said in English. "Didn't they tell you? It was dying, and we took it back to nurse from a wild mare."

"Well, that's too bad. But spring is a long time away. We'll think of something by then. Now get the pinto and do as I say."

The boy went out, smoldering. Wildwing pulling a plow? Never! Not as long as he lived would he allow that. There were plenty of broomtails like the pinto for such work. No, Wildwing would be a racer like his grandfather's horse, Raven.

He got the pinto and rode it at a trot to the

spring. As the animal drank, he noticed its resemblance to Storm. The same large bony head, curved nose, coarse mane and knobby legs. Like the mare, it was nervous, with rolling eyes that were always looking for trouble. Though he had never liked the pinto, he felt sorry for it now. But it was quick and crafty, and might well throw a strange rider like Tall Man. He would wait and see how things went. At a gallop, he could be out to the highway without wasting much time.

Back at the cabin, he found that Gray Wolf had changed his mind. The pinto was to be hitched to the wagon. They were all to go to see the new car. "Good," thought Bronze Feather, "they will not need me," and went to get the ancient harness. When all was ready he handed the reins to his father.

"No, you lead him," said Gray Wolf and climbed up to join Running Water on the wagon seat.

"I would rather not go."

"My son, I have spoken!" The words in Arapahoe had authority.

Little Bud came round the side of the wagon

and touched her brother's arm. "I wish you would come—and our mother wishes it too," she said in a low voice. "The mare will care for the colt; we saw how she fought for him. Do not worry."

Bronze Feather scowled. "All right. But remember—speak English."

"O.K.," said Little Bud.

The trail crossed bare rock ledge. The wagon banged and jolted, and then sank into sandy shale. At a huge boulder that marked the halfway point they stopped to let the pinto rest. It was a place of silence and majestic beauty, but as the pinto lowered his head to graze, sudden sounds broke the stillness. Long labored grinding, broken by rapid explosions. Then the grinding sound again.

"Must be a big truck," said Gray Wolf, standing up in the wagon.

"Sounds like a bulldozer. Maybe they're fixing the road," suggested Little Bud.

The wagon creaked on, but when they reached the highway there was no sign of Tall Man or the car. The grinding noise had stopped. An odor of burning oil hung in the air.

90

"Go down around the bend where we can see ahead. That truck might be holding up the car," said Gray Wolf.

But at the bend their way was blocked. Steam rose in a cloud from the radiator of a big pale blue automobile. Its fenders were missing, which gave it an odd naked look, as if the wheels had been placed there by mistake. The hood was raised and the plump face of the half-breed Tall Man looked up from the inward depths of the motor. "Heated up," he said. "Awful climb up here. All it needs is some water."

While the others stared at the car, Gray Wolf jumped down from the wagon and joined Tall Man in the inspection of the motor.

"It looks like the cars the boys around town race with," whispered Little Bud to her brother.

"That's what it is, I think. A hot-rod."

Bronze Feather tied the pinto to a bush, and they walked around to the back of the car.

"Look, the top is gone too," exclaimed Little Bud.

"Sure, they strip them down for racing."

Running Water had not moved from her seat in the wagon. Her gentle face showed neither surprise nor disappointment. If the car would not move, they would go back with the pinto and the wagon, and that would be the end of this foolishness.

"All it needs is some water," Tall Man repeated.

Gray Wolf climbed out from the driver's seat. "That would take too long. The pinto can pull it up to the wagon trail."

This solution seemed as good as any. Little Bud led the pinto while the men pushed. The highway being level here, the car moved ahead without much trouble. It was towed to the entrance of the wagon trail. Gray Wolf got behind the steering wheel and stepped on the starter. It whirred dismally. The motor coughed once, and then died.

Tall Man kept smiling. "It's still hot. Better not try it without water. I'll take you home in the wagon and ride the pinto back."

"Water nothing! There's no gas in the tank!" exclaimed Gray Wolf. "The gauge says zero!"

Tall Man shrugged. "Oh, that's not working."

Back at the cabin an argument started as to

whether the old saddle was to be included in the deal, but here Gray Wolf was stubborn. No saddle. Tall Man could ride the pinto bareback. It was enough that he was getting the bridle.

The pinto was no bargain. He was still half wild. Only Gray Wolf and Bronze Feather had ridden him, but when handled right he was a good and willing worker. When not in use, he was kept staked by a rope in the meadow to keep him from straying. Now, unhitched from the wagon and free of the harness, he wheeled around Bronze Feather, who held him by the bridle while Tall Man mounted.

The pinto trembled. His ears lay flat. His eyes rolled white. Then, with a sudden unaccountable grace, his body buckled, and Tall Man sailed over his head. The rider got up, still smiling. His next attempt ended in the same way, except that he hung on longer and slid, instead of being hurled, to the ground.

"You didn't tell me he was a bucker!" he shouted.

"He isn't. Never saw him buck before," replied

Gray Wolf truthfully. "Try him again. He's skittish with strangers."

But now, furious with this game, the pinto broke loose and fled to the meadow. There was no use in pursuit, for once free he would stay well out of reach.

Tall Man said, "That horse is no good. I can't fool with him. I want cash money for the car."

Running Water had watched all this from the cabin doorway. Now she spoke in slow careful English. "The car is not good either. *We* have not time to fool with *it*." Having most of Gray Wolf's pay in her skirt pocket, she meant to keep it, for there was no telling when there would be more.

Tall Man looked at her with malice in his eyes. "You, a woman, run this house?"

"Yes," replied Running Water, "for there is no one else to do it. You have tricked my husband, but the thing has turned on you." She went into the cabin and began to prepare a meal. Despite her words, there would be food and lodging for Tall Man until he could pick up a ride with some truck or car passing on the highway.

While the men sat smoking, Bronze Feather sauntered toward the pines, where he had left his rifle. The odor of food wafting from the cabin reminded him that he had not eaten that day. But to sit through a long meal with much talk would be a waste of time. As he stood thinking about it, Little Bud came out with a packet in her hand.

"I have brought some bread and cheese," she said in Arapahoe. "I knew you were anxious to go. Our mother sent it," she said with a smile.

Bronze Feather took the packet and picked up his gun. "Thank our mother," he said, and added with a twinkle in his eyes, "Do not let our father race the car on the highway. The law says only sixty miles an hour."

"It needs only water," laughed Little Bud and skipped away.

THE PINTO GONE

Wildwing seemed to be alone in the grotto.

Coming down the steep slope above the spring, Bronze Feather saw the tawny head bobbing above the weeds, weaving in and out among the bushes and trees—a perfect target for the panther.

Where was Storm? Why did she allow the colt to wander alone when she must *know* the big cat was around? Perhaps she could not be trusted after all. The boy moved swiftly to the bottom of the grotto and in his indignation walked out in full sight of the colt.

Wildwing saw him at once and came toward him, nose reached out, eyes big with friendly curi-

osity. It happened so naturally that Bronze Feather could hardly believe they had ever been separated. His hands smoothed and caressed the velvety neck and face, tidying the brush of mane. All the while he kept talking in a half-whisper. "You remember me, little one—you are not *really* wild, like the others. . . . But you must be careful. Stay with Storm, or the panther will come creeping."

Wildwing rubbed his head along the protecting arms, lipped at the brass buttons on the blue denim jacket and at the brim of the dusty sombrero. The boy went on whispering, loving and scolding at the same time. Now the colt belonged to him again. The long wait was over.

A branch snapped. Bronze Feather looked up and saw the mare. She was grazing a little distance away, her head toward the pass. She turned now and then, but there was no fear in her movements. She made no effort to conceal herself, or to warn the colt. A wave of gratitude came over him. She was taking care of Wildwing. He would never mistrust her again.

Then suddenly she snorted. The sound was imperative—commanding. The colt obeyed at once, flying to her with long-legged leaps.

"The Great Spirit Above watches over them. I have no need to worry," the boy thought reverently.

It was late afternoon when he reached the cabin. Tall Man was gone, and Gray Wolf, sitting on the doorstep, seemed to have forgotten all about the car, and spoke of the corn crop and the weather.

Bronze Feather went to look for the pinto. Finding no trace of the horse, he began to worry. The dangling reins of the bridle might trip and throw an animal going over rough country. He went out again the next morning, this time with Little Bud. In the meadow they saw no clear hoofmarks until they reached the far end where the grass thinned into sand. The pinto had headed for open country, for the tracks turned west and crossed the highway just above the wagon trail.

The blue convertible looked faded and desolate

under the blazing sun. But something about it was different. It seemed lower, almost sunk into the earth.

"What has happened to it?" exclaimed Little Bud, shading her eyes with her hand.

"Happened! The wheels are gone!" shouted her brother.

Stripped of everything movable, the hulk sat squat on the ground, the empty shells of its headlights making two round dark eyes. Seat cushions, spare tire, battery, spark plugs—all were gone.

The twins stared at it in silence. "Now we *must*

find the pinto," Bronze Feather said as they walked slowly away. All afternoon they searched, coming home toward sunset. It seemed likely to them that the pinto had gone to join the wild horses, but their mother was sure Tall Man had captured him.

"Has he not taken the very wheels from the car? What more proof is needed of his craftiness?" she said.

A week passed, and still the pinto did not return. Bronze Feather made his daily morning visits to the grotto and came back to work in the cornfield or the garden. Little Bud had gone with him twice, and gave glowing accounts of Wildwing.

"You cannot believe how he has grown! And the mare is not afraid; she grazed near us when we were with the colt."

Running Water smiled at her eagerness. "You have much faith, you and your brother—but someday I fear they will be gone. For wild horses wander, there is no knowing where they will be from one day to the next. When the graze is gone in one place, they move to another."

"We have thought of that, and we are worried," replied Little Bud. "They have nothing to eat in the grotto now." She did not mention that the colt and mare were already getting the beet and carrot thinnings from the garden, as well as some of the young corn.

The mother went on with her work. She was stitching colored beads to a new doeskin jacket, arranging them in small beautiful patterns. She took pride in her work and it found a ready sale at the Indian Crafts Center.

"Will you sell this one?" asked Little Bud.

"I had thought to. Also the four pairs of beaded moccasins. It is well that our grandfather knows the art of tanning deer hides. When he comes to visit us he will teach Bronze Feather how to do it. But your brother has not gotten a deer in a long time," she added, looking up.

Little Bud was silent, and Running Water went on. "With the pinto gone, it will be a long walk to town. Your father searched for him again today. He might better have looked for Tall Man."

Little Bud walked slowly toward the garden. Bronze Feather was pulling weeds from the bean rows.

"I have been thinking . . ." she began, and stopped.

"It is not unusual to think," teased Bronze Feather.

"Well—if Storm and Wildwing had enough to eat, maybe they would not leave with the stallion and the others. Maybe Wildwing could be tamed."

"Who says they are *leaving?*" demanded Bronze Feather.

"Our mother says they may leave at any time. You also have been concerned about that."

"But we are taming them *now*. Both of them!"

"But what if they go away?" said Little Bud impatiently.

Bronze Feather pulled a weed and shook the earth from its roots.

"My plan is to take them both. If we keep feeding them they may stay in the grotto until—until, well, they might just stay."

104

Gray Wolf was stunned by the loss of the blue convertible. When he learned what had happened to it, he went up to gaze at it and grieve. Being something of a mechanic, he had planned to work on the motor and perhaps repaint the body. Without fenders it had seemed racy and rakish, but without wheels there was no hope for the fulfillment of his dream of owning a big car. He took to visiting it in the afternoons, and often spent hours seated behind the steering wheel, pushing the brake in and out, handling the gearshift as though he were really driving.

Little Bud saw him there one day when she was picking wild berries, and went away without speaking. Everyone, she thought, longed for something they did not have. Even the pinto had been dissatisfied with his lot.

Then one day Gray Wolf announced that he had another job. A truckman he knew had passed on the road and had offered him work in a garage as a handyman. He left the next day, the man having arranged to pick him up at the wagon-trail crossing. Running Water was pleased, for Gray Wolf had been restless and unhappy in the quiet mountain retreat.

June edged into July. The days were hot and windy, and though gray fleeces sometimes massed over the mountains, they kept their distance and gave no promise of rain. Leaves curled on the trees and the grass withered. Only the weeds thrived, and now they were a blessing to Bronze Feather, who gathered them into a burlap bag along with a few carrots and some cornstalks. The mare and the colt had come to expect and wait for this early morning feeding. At first only Wildwing came hurrying to the feast handed out from the bag. While he stood munching the greens, Storm watched, not quite certain of the wisdom of coming so near to a human. But each morning she edged nearer. The boy was patient but firm.

"You must take it from my hand," he told her. "See how the colt eats—he is not afraid."

Storm's ears flicked backward and forward as her nostrils caught the scent of the carrot he held out. She had never been so close before. Then her long neck reached out. She snatched the carrot and backed away to eat it. Bronze Feather grinned. She would soon be tamed.

He watched the tracks around the spring in the grotto. When there were no fresh tramplings he knew that the stallion and his band had not come, and guessed that they were sometimes watering farther west in the pass. But to lose Wildwing now was unthinkable, and as for Storm, she belonged to him and not to the stallion, who had a whole band of mares. True, she was no beauty, but she was wise and courageous, and better-tempered than the pinto. With patience she could be tamed and trained to take his place.

How this could be accomplished he had no clear idea, but that evening he began felling trees and trimming off branches. He had decided to build a corral near the cabin spring where rock walls formed a deep bay. There was both shade and shelter from rain, under an overhanging cliff. A few trees and bushes grew among the crevices. It was a perfect place for a corral.

Little Bud helped him, and when they found

that the shallow soil offered no footing for upright poles they piled brush across the narrow entrance. It was a way of fence building that their grandfather had taught them. Piled high, the brush made a bristling wall, not easily moved. A small space was left for a barway or entrance, but Bronze Feather dug many holes with a shovel before he found a place to set the posts.

At last the corral was finished; the long poles for the bars, smoothed of their notches, were ready to set in place. It was dusk and the twins were very tired as they walked up the trail toward the cabin. "I wish our grandfather could see it," said Bronze Feather.

The lamp was lighted in the cabin and Running Water was packing a bundle.

"You have worked late," she said. "But when we have eaten we must go to rest, for I have been thinking that I would take my things to the town tomorrow. It will be best to rise early and be on my way before the sun is hot."

"You will walk—all that distance?" exclaimed Little Bud.

"With no horse, I must do what I can," replied their mother. "And it is not so far. I will stay with our kin the first night, and return in four days."

"Let me go with you to help carry the things," said Little Bud quickly. She was feeling a little guilty for having spent all her evenings down at the corral.

"No. It is better that you stay here. Your brother is so busy with the foal that he will forget about the cow and the garden and the corn." There was no sharpness in Running Water's voice, only resignation.

Bronze Feather was silent. What their mother said was true. He *had* spent much of his time away from duties. "Must you go now?" he said at last. "If you wait, perhaps the pinto will come back."

"I have waited. But I cannot wait any longer, and this is the best time to go."

When the first streak of dawn paled the stars Running Water set off from the cabin with the jacket and the moccasins and some food in a bundle which she carried on her back. It did not seem heavy, nor was she disheartened by the long journey, for she liked to walk, and would not have anyone come with her even as far as the highway.

"If you see our grandfather, tell him we long to hear his stories," Little Bud called after her.

When their mother's tall figure had disappeared around a bend the girl went back to the cabin. It seemed gloomy and cheerless in the early morning light. But hearing Bronze Feather stir in the back room, she set food on the table. "How brave our mother is," she thought. "We must take good care of the garden and the cornfield while she is away."

By the time she had milked the cow and turned her loose in the meadow, Bronze Feather was ready with the usual bag of greens for the horses. "We cannot take many more carrots," he said, lifting the bag to his shoulder.

Little Bud made a circle in the dust with her moccasin. "Maybe we should not go to the grotto today," she said. "There is much work to be——"

A sudden high-pitched scream sounded and resounded from the canyon. It came twice, the last one seeming farther away and more of a wail than a scream.

They ran down the trail. At the spring, Bronze Feather slipped the cumbersome bag from his shoulder. "That was the panther—I must go quickly." He dashed ahead, clutching his gun.

NO CARROTS?

The way to the grotto seemed endless. As well as Bronze Feather knew every rock and boulder, they now seemed to move, and to keep moving ahead. His feet pounded the sand. His lungs gulped the air. His mind was a blank except for one image, the long tawny body of the panther. He slowed to a trot, to a walk, and then ran again.

Now the cat was crouching—ready for the leap. He himself gave a leap—over the old battered litter. The sight of it cheered him; he was almost at the grotto. He became all caution, snaking his way over the bulging rock ledge above. At the grotto entrance he waited and listened. Then moved a few steps forward, his gun up and ready.

All was quiet. He crept down, watching his footing, sliding through branches, brushing lightly among leaves. Ready as he was, the patch of tawny color that moved just ahead made him tremble. He leveled his gun, his finger on the trigger.

Wildwing peered at him through the green.

The colt nickered and came forward, but the boy stood as if rooted to the ground. He had almost —the thought made him dizzy. He leaned against a tree for support. His eyes closed and then opened and then closed again. Wildwing was nuzzling into his jacket pocket, bunting him gently as if to remind him that he, Wildwing, was there and waiting.

Bronze Feather gripped the colt in a bearlike hug. "Wildwing—forgive me——"

Storm had been watching from a little distance. Now she came up, eying the scene curiously. But something was wrong. There was no smell of carrots or fresh greens. She dropped her head and began lipping at a fern.

At last the boy spoke to them, trying to explain that their meal was coming. They had only to wait until he could go back to get it. With the tension past, he felt rather foolish. He had come armed with a gun, instead of carrots!

Storm had not needed his protection. She knew the ways of the big cat and was always on guard. With a colt to protect, she was unusually careful, testing the air constantly for any scent of an enemy. She had heard the panther's cry, and knew that it was a long distance away, and that the cat was not hunting. For it hunted in silence, leaping upon its prey without warning.

Bronze Feather began climbing back toward the canyon. To his surprise, the colt came scrambling behind. They arrived at the narrow entrance together, and when the boy looked back and saw Storm's head bobbing through the branches he suddenly dared to hope for the impossible. They might come all the way out. *They might even fol-*

low him home! Now would be his chance. If only he had brought the burlap bag!

Little Bud would bring it, he was certain, but that might take a long time, for the bag was heavy. She was still not in sight. Would mare and colt wait?

"Follow—please follow," whispered Bronze Feather, not daring to look back again. He ran down the rock ledge and began walking up the canyon at a snail's pace. "They must come of their own will," he kept saying to himself.

But now he saw Little Bud far in the distance. He went slowly on. When he saw her again, he gave the call of the whippoorwill. She would know its meaning; to advance without showing herself, the way they used the signal in their games.

He looked back. Storm had stopped at the foot of the rock ledge with head up, ears forward and nostrils wide open. The colt stood beside her. The boy knew it was foolish to hope they would follow him—he had nothing to offer them, and there was no graze in the canyon. He trudged on.

Just then a carrot was thrown out from behind a boulder ahead. There was another beyond it, and a bit of green that looked like a cornstalk beyond that. Bronze Feather grinned. Only Little Bud would have thought of such a trick. As he stooped to pick up the carrot she spoke to him from behind the rock.

"I heard your call, and then I saw the horses following you. But the bag was heavy, so I began throwing some of the corn and carrots out. I still have some left. You will find them all the way along."

"That was wise," replied her brother. "You go ahead. Maybe we can get them to follow us all the way home."

Storm, having scented food, came eagerly forward with the colt at her heels. Each took a carrot from Bronze Feather's hand. Step by step they moved ahead, Little Bud leading, the others following, and the boy thinking that this was almost too easy. But the real test would come where the trail led up from the canyon.

As they went along Little Bud began putting some of the corn and carrots back into the bag to be handed out later, when the supply on the ground had ended. It was a slow journey—Wildwing nibbling and gnawing at the carrots Bronze Feather rationed out to him, Storm following, a comic figure with a stalk held crosswise in her mouth. Sometimes she stopped to look back, as if doubting the wisdom of going so far from her range and her companions. Whenever she hesitated the boy hurried the colt ahead, feeling sure that she would follow. And follow she did, right past the grove of cottonwoods and around the bend and up the trail toward the corral.

Little Bud walked ahead, doling the food out sparingly. The choicest carrots were dropped at the entrance to the corral, and scattered here and there inside. The bars to the opening were in place, ready to be closed. She stood beside them and waited for the procession to come up the slope.

Slowly they came, Bronze Feather speaking to the horses in low soothing tones. But his face was grim and his legs were shaking as he neared the corral. Still, they had come up from the canyon without hesitation, maybe they would still follow. . . . He stepped through the barway, one hand resting lightly on the colt's brush of mane, the other holding a carrot up to the small muzzle. Once inside, he felt better, and led his captive to the far end of the corral.

Storm stopped at the entrance, ears forward, nostrils flared wide. She took one step and grasped the nearest carrot from the ground. While she munched it, Bronze Feather felt the sweat run down his face. Now she was inside and had snatched at a cornstalk. At that instant Little Bud slid the top pole of the bars into place, and the next instant Storm had wheeled and sailed over it like a great dark bird.

The mare ran a little way down the trail and then turned, head flung high, her eyes rolling white. A screeching whinny came from her throat. Wild-wing answered, and as Bronze Feather ran to help his sister put the other poles in place, the colt followed. Finding himself separated from the mare,

118

he became frantic, neighing wildly, pawing at the bars and at the brush.

"Watch out for the mare! Keep out of her way!" shouted Bronze Feather.

Little Bud scrambled up to the top of a rock while her brother tried to calm the colt. But now food and soft words were spurned. Wildwing wanted his mother. Neigh answered neigh, until the forest rang with their cries.

"Run—she is coming!" screamed Little Bud.

Storm came over the bars with ears flat and teeth bared, a fury of rage and power. There was only an instant of time, but Bronze Feather was quick. With one leap he made the branch of a tree, scrambled up, and pulled himself to a narrow rock rim. There he balanced for a moment, and then his hand found a root. The height was nothing, but still he felt dizzy. He rested against the rock and let the dizziness pass and then turned to look down.

In the center of the corral stood the mare, chewing calmly at a cornstalk while Wildwing nursed at her side.

"So that was it," he muttered, and remembered

that the colt had not nursed in all the long way up from the canyon. He waved to Little Bud, who was now perched on the bars, and then looked for a way to get down without dropping back into the corral. Finding none, he decided to chance it.

Storm paid no attention when he passed, and later, when the colt sprawled in the shade of the rock cliff, she stood dozing beside him like an old farmhorse. Awkward, big-headed, and scrawny, she had proved her mettle and her faithfulness. The twins, sitting on the bars, looked at her with admiration. "And think—she is not even the colt's true mother!" exclaimed Little Bud.

The whole thing was a miracle. They could hardly believe what their eyes saw—two *wild horses*, brought home without rope or halter. Such a thing had never been done by anyone in the family, not even Long Bow, their grandfather.

"They will not be hard to tame. We will have two good horses," mused Bronze Feather. "You did not see the stallion, but he was beautiful, with much dark mane and a great flowing tail. Wildwing will look just like him." The boy's eyes became dreamy, but suddenly he sat up straight. "We forgot water! The mare must be thirsty."

Little Bud looked at him thoughtfully. "We forgot something else. *What will they eat?*"

"Oh, we will find something," replied her brother lightly. He jumped to the ground and they went up to the cabin, where they found an old tub. On their way back to the corral they stopped at the garden. Dusk had fallen, so they saw little of what they gathered, but they emptied a heaping tubful of greens over the bars. Then back to the spring to fill the tub with water. Full darkness had come by the time they had tugged it under the bars, called good night to their captives, and trudged back up the trail, weary but happy.

A distant storm muttered and growled over the mountains.

Little Bud milked the cow by the light of the lantern. Bronze Feather, gathering firewood, smiled as he heard her singing. He made fires in the cookstove and in the fireplace. It was a happy evening. They ate largely of hot corn bread and the meat and vegetable stew their mother had thoughtfully prepared for them. When the rain came it fell steadily on the roof, with no thunder or lightning.

After supper they stretched out before the fireplace.

"Only think," said Bronze Feather, "we have them both—the colt and the mare."

"But Storm leaps the bars. She may go back."

"She will not go far if Wildwing cannot follow." Bronze Feather yawned and then suddenly sat up. "My gun! I left it in the canyon when I began picking up the carrots. It got in my way."

"You can get it tomorrow," said Little Bud, not much concerned.

"But the colt is penned up. If the panther should come—" He got up and went to the door. The night was black and he was very tired. He went back to the fire.

It rained all night, a steady downpour that made tiny streams overflow, filled brooks and washes and sent them swirling down ravines and canyons. The cabin yard was a lake in the morning. Bronze Feather splashed through it and raced down to the corral. A few small pools of water had gathered here and there in hollows, but the place under the cliff was dry. He had picked a good spot for the corral, he thought as he swung up onto the bars.

Wildwing and Storm were cleaning up the last bits of the corn and carrots. Now, seeing him, they came to find what new bounty he had to offer. He spoke to them, making promises of good things to come if they would behave well and become trustworthy.

"You must be re-li-able," he said in English. "I learned that word in school. It's English, not Arapahoe. You will learn English next winter when we go back to our other place."

Mare and colt listened, their ears moving backward and forward as if they understood what he was saying. Wildwing came up to have his head scratched. Storm followed. Now she was within easy reach of his hand. She had never been so close before—no human had ever touched her. He reached out and brushed his fingers lightly over her shaggy back. The hide trembled as if she were shaking off a fly. He tried it again, this time with a firmer motion, and felt the sharp swish of her tail. But she had not moved or shown fear at his touch. Bronze Feather was elated. She would soon be tamed.

But walking back toward the cabin, he began to worry. What would he feed them today? Storm could of course go over the bars if she wanted to, but that was no way to tame a horse. It was the promise of food that had lured them away from their wild range. *He* was the one who had to be reliable. They were his responsibility now.

He spoke of it to Little Bud, and when the cow had been milked they went out to the cornfield together. The rows were tasseling out in fringes of silk that hung from the young ears on the stalks. Bronze Feather slit one open. The small kernels were still soft and white, but in time they would be firm and golden in color. That was the time for the harvest. To take them now would mean the loss of the corn meal that was part of the family's winter food supply.

He waved his arm in a circle. "All of this land, and we planted so little."

"When you were hoeing it, you thought we had planted too much," teased Little Bud.

They walked along, taking a stalk here and there, selecting the ones with the fewest ears. From the garden, beets, squash, carrots and beans found their way into the burlap bag.

"What will we feed them tomorrow?" asked Little Bud, looking at the gaps in the rows.

"I do not know," replied her brother briefly.

They went to the corral, and as they watched the new pile of food disappear, their faces grew sober and worried.

"Maybe they would eat leaves," suggested Little Bud. "There are many trees."

"Horses do not like leaves. We must think of some other way. I will think about it while I go to the canyon to get my gun."

When Bronze Feather was gone, his sister walked slowly back toward the cabin, stopping at the spring to pick up the water jugs she had left there. She opened the cabin door. How untidy the room looked! Dishes unwashed, floor unswept, everything out of place. She was no better at keeping things in order than her brother was, it seemed. But now there was time. She grabbed the broom and set to work, and when Bronze Feather came back the cabin was tidy and cheerful.

"Your gun was not rusty with the rain?" she asked when he came in with a pair of limp grouse over his shoulder.

"No, but the foolish birds could have been killed with a pebble, for they walked directly in my path." His voice seemed so despondent that Little Bud turned to look at him.

"What has happened?" she asked.

"The mare has leaped the bars again."

"But that is good!" exclaimed Little Bud. "She will find graze and then go back. You worry too much. See, I have food ready. Let us eat instead of worrying." Little Bud was determined to be cheerful.

"She will break her legs if she keeps jumping. Then I will have to shoot her," was Bronze Feather's gloomy reply.

"Did you see where she went?"

"No. But she did not go to the canyon, for I saw no tracks. There is no knowing what she will do. But I will not give up the colt."

When they had eaten, Bronze Feather cleaned and oiled his gun. Little Bud plucked the grouse and set them to boil on the stove. Then she went out to the garden to get vegetables.

The pale sun had disappeared behind banks of fog that rolled up from the canyon and drifted among the pines, wrapping them in soft veils of gray. She bent over the bean rows. There were sharp oval hoofmarks in the wet earth. They circled the plants and led off toward the cornfield. She followed them. Some of the stalks had been trampled, some torn up by the roots.

Little Bud gazed around, numb with fright.

HAY! OATS!

Little Bud ran through the corn. Storm was gone —swallowed up in the fog, but it was easy to follow her destructive course. The tracks led to the end of the field, where she had apparently leaped the low wire fence.

"She will come back. We cannot keep her out," the girl whispered to herself. She walked slowly back through the dripping rows, straightening a stalk here and there, trampling the earth back into place around the roots. Then suddenly she ran, and came panting into the cabin.

"The corn—the mare has been in the corn!"

Bronze Feather laid his gun down. They stared

at each other with stricken faces. Then they were out, racing along the trail toward the corral. Wildwing's cries came through the fog. He was frantic, pawing at the bars, leaping at the brush. They stayed a moment to comfort him and then ran to the cornfield.

But as they hurried up and down the rows, shouting and whistling in an effort to frighten the mare, the fog thickened and dusk settled down. It was hopeless, they knew. She would come back at night, or at any time she chose. They gathered a few vegetables and went back to the cabin, tired and wet and discouraged.

Bronze Feather got the cow from the meadow and brought in wood for the fires. They went about their work in silence, but when Little Bud was milking, her brother came out and leaned on the corral posts.

"I have brought this trouble," he began slowly. "Our mother was right, but I would not listen to her. I wanted Wildwing more than anything in all the world. But everything I did was for myself.

I deceived the hunters, and then left my work to spend my time in the grotto. Now I am punished. . . ." He bowed his head on his folded arms.

"It was not your fault only. I was as much to blame," Little Bud said gently. "We could not know this would happen, and we needed a horse."

"But this one is wild! She will destroy the garden and the corn long before we can tame her. In one night she can trample it down." Bronze Feather began pacing back and forth. Suddenly he stopped.

"I have decided. I will give Wildwing up. It is the only way. When the mare comes back I will open the bars and set them both free."

"Then they will both go to the cornfield!" cried Little Bud.

"I will take them back to the grotto."

"Tonight? And pull the last of the carrots? We had better stay up all night and guard the field," replied Little Bud. She got to her feet and picked up the milk pail.

A thundering BOOM echoed and re-echoed around them.

The sound seemed to come from the west, as if two cliffs had crashed together or an avalanche had torn a mountain apart.

"What was that?" whispered Little Bud.

Bronze Feather shook his head. "I don't know. It was not thunder."

They stood listening. All was quiet except for the dripping from the trees. "I think it was something on the highway," said Bronze Feather at last. "I heard a sound like a motor just before that."

"Maybe a car went over the cliff. In this fog they could not see." Little Bud shivered.

"That may be," replied Bronze Feather.

They listened again, but there was no sound.

Bronze Feather picked up the lantern, and they went to the cabin door.

"Should we go out to the highway?" asked Little Bud.

"I think so. But first I will go down to the corral."

The lantern bobbed down the trail. In a few minutes Bronze Feather was back with the news that Storm was in the corral again.

"I saw them together, they were both under the rock shelter. Now let us go."

They trotted along the wagon trail, Bronze Feather ahead with the lantern. Long before reaching the highway they heard faint muffled voices and saw fog-dimmed lights below. They slowed to a walk, and then trotted again.

"Something has happened at the cliff, I think," Bronze Feather said.

As they approached the highway, Little Bud touched her brother's arm. "I will wait here at this rock. It is better for you to go alone."

"Then do not move, or I will not find you. And keep the lantern. I will not need it," said Bronze Feather, and disappeared into the fog.

He moved slowly and carefully, and soon felt the hard surface of the highway under his feet. Lights swung about and voices shouted. Then his outstretched hand felt the cold touch of wet metal. A great bulky shape seemed to have risen out of nowhere. He felt along its wet surface. It was a car, there was no doubt of that. Then his hand touched something rounded and greasy. The bare hub ends of an axle—a car without wheels!

The blue convertible! But how could it be here —in the middle of the highway?

He left it and, picking his way ahead, went toward the dim lights that bobbed back and forth. He went slowly, remembering that there was not much space between the road and the cliff.

A man's voice came out of the fog. "The load's lost. That's for sure."

"Who cares?" came the reply. "We might both be down there on top of it! I'd rather camp up here than down there! The truck's just balancing on the edge."

"What was that thing we hit? Can't make it out —up here in the wilderness!"

"Wait till the boss hears this!"

"I can't wait. Tell me now."

Bronze Feather listened for a long time. Gradually the fog began to lift. A star appeared here and there in the sky. The flares that had been placed on the highway to warn other traffic burned more brightly, and for the first time he saw the vast bulk of the truck cab. It stood dimly outlined against the sky like a butte in the canyon, its smashed headlights pointed upward, its huge front wheels apparently caught on the edge of the cliff.

The real damage, judging from the truckmen's talk, had been done to the load it had carried. *Ten tons of baled hay and bags of oats* on their way to a ranch in the valley below.

Hay! Oats! Bronze Feather felt as if he were choking, and backed quickly behind a boulder lest they should hear his heart beating.

"Hay—oats—" he kept whispering and shook with silent laughter. Oh, it was down in a deep chasm, hundreds of feet below the highway; but he would get it; carry it up straw by straw, grain by grain. He knew the way down. He would work at it day and night. . . . He hugged himself, rocking backward and forward like a mechanical toy.

Now the truckmen had walked over to look at the cause of the wreck—the mass of twisted tangled metal, the hot-rod that had once been the blue convertible. Their flashlights played upon the road bank and then back to the highway.

"That's where it was—up on the ledge," one of them said. "See the slide marks?"

"Yeh, the heavy rain must have made it come down. But how in the name of time did that thing get up here in the mountains?"

"Beats me. Look, Bill, no wheels! What kind of deal *is* this?"

Bronze Feather slid back into the deep shadows and making a wide circle, came out on the wagon trail. There was no light, but he knew that Little Bud was nearby, and gave the soft call of the owl. The reply came at once, and when she met him she carried a darkened lantern. They walked swiftly away.

When they had gone a little distance Bronze Feather said, "You heard the men speaking. Did you hear what they said?"

"Yes," replied his sister softly, "they spoke of hay and oats. The Great Spirit Above has sent it to us, I think."

"But tons and tons of it! Enough for fifty horses!"

"Do not be too sure. They might come and get it up again."

"They can never get it up. I know where it fell—down into the great chasm. The hay is scattered, the bags of oats——" Bronze Feather made a sweeping motion with his arms. Then, as if first realizing the wonder of it, he did two somersaults, leaped up to grasp an overhanging branch, swung on it, and bounced down as if on springs.

"There is one trouble," he explained. "Can you guess what it is?"

Little Bud laughed. "That you will break your legs—with your leapings in the dark."

"No! That I cannot shout and yell. And I cannot, because the men must not hear us. The cause of the wreck was our father's old car. It was in the road."

Little Bud walked with head down, as if lost in

deep thought. A full moon rose over the trees, edging their leaves with silver.

"Bronze Feather . . ."

"What is it? You are not pleased with what has happened?" asked her brother.

"Yes, you know I am. But, remember, you spoke awhile ago about, well, being selfish, and how you were punished?"

"Mmm . . . But now I know I was mistaken," replied Bronze Feather.

"How do you know? It was our father's car that made the trouble for these men. Very bad trouble. It is not right that we should profit by that and give them nothing in return. I think we should go back and offer them food and lodging for the night. If we are not selfish, things may come out right this time. The Great Spirit may have given us this chance."

Bronze Feather pulled at a twig along the road and stripped its leaves. "But they are white men. Their ways are different from ours. They would not understand."

"Now you are speaking like our grandfather.

Our mother would not agree," said Little Bud. "She has taught us to be kind to everyone. She would be pleased if we offered to help them. If you will not come, I will go back alone."

Bronze Feather knew there was no shaking his twin once her mind was made up, so he followed her when she turned back. There was no need for the lantern now; a brilliant moon shone over the silent plateau and edged with silver the long rolls of fog that hung over the distant ridges to the west.

The two men were leaning against a rock near their truck. They seemed surprised when Bronze Feather and Little Bud came toward them.

"Well—where did you come from?" said one.

"We live near here," replied Bronze Feather in English. "We heard a loud noise——"

The men grinned. "I'll say. We hit that old wreck in the fog. Lucky we weren't killed. Bill, here, got his arm banged up, but that's all."

"Except for the load. Don't forget that, Les," exclaimed Bill. "Ten tons of hay and oats—all gone over the cliff!"

The men seemed to be friendly and talkative, but Little Bud noticed that the one named Bill kept his arm held across his chest.

"Does your arm hurt?" she asked timidly.

"Naw, it's nothing. Just a bruise," replied Bill.

Little Bud glanced at her brother and, knowing that he would not help her out, went bravely on. "We have a cabin up there. You are welcome to stay there tonight, if you would like."

"Gee, thanks, that's very nice of you," said Les, "but we've got to stay here with the truck. She's hanging over the cliff by her toenails, and if she slides, we want to be here."

"All night?"

"Guess so. Or until someone comes along the road. Not much traffic here, I guess. We've got a two-way radio in the truck cab, but you'd have to be nuts to get into it now, the way she's balanced," Les said with an air of finality.

Bronze Feather had been walking around the front of the truck, kneeling now and then to examine the position of the huge front wheels. All that held them was an upthrust ledge of rock which was locked behind them. The monster trailer hung almost perpendicular, and, as Bill explained, "The only thing that saved us was getting rid of the load. Slid right off the back. All insured, though," he added with satisfaction.

"Will you haul it up—the hay and the oats?" asked Bronze Feather quickly.

"We couldn't. It's all busted to pieces. And no way to get down there—must be over two hundred feet, from what we could see with our flashlights. Wouldn't pay to bother with it."

The boy continued his investigation of the truck wheels, leaving Little Bud to talk with the men.

"Does your father have a truck?" Bill asked her.

Little Bud smiled and shook her head. "Only a wagon, but our pinto ran away, so now we must walk." She hesitated and then went on. "If you are hungry, I could bring some food and coffee."

"Now you're talking." Les grinned. "We sure could use some hot coffee."

"Yeh, for our nerves," added Bill. "My legs are still wobbly."

"O.K. I'll be right back," said Little Bud, happy to be able to make some repayment for their newly found riches.

"Sure you're not afraid?" asked Les, handing her his flashlight.

"Nothing to be afraid of," laughed Little Bud and trotted away.

The men yawned and stretched. "It's going to be a long night. Only ten now," Bill said, looking at his wrist watch.

"How's your arm?"

"It's beginning to get sore. Wish I could see a doctor. What gets me—we've got that radio. Could have someone out here by just turning a switch!"

Bronze Feather stood at the open truck door, which hung aslant on its smashed hinges. "What switch? Which one is it?" he asked, looking at the knobs and buttons on the panel.

Bill turned his flashlight on the panel. "There are two switches. One on that box, and one on the earphone—that thing with the twisted cord. That little light turns red when the circuit is open."

"But how does it work?" asked Bronze Feather.

Bill looked at him sharply. "Why do you want to know?"

"Nothing. I just never saw one before. Is it like a telephone?"

"Same idea. You turn on the switches, and when you have contact, when the thing begins to crackle, you begin to talk. In our outfit we say the number of the truck. Like this one is number fifteen, and then you give your location. Someone will answer and you tell him what you want. When you're finished you turn off the switches. Nothing to it. But we can't risk touching anything now. So don't get near it," Bill said firmly.

The boy nodded and sauntered away, his face calm, but his mind seething with excitement. Maybe he could do something to help too. Little Bud had gone to get food and coffee. She was doing her part. He had done nothing. There was no danger of the truck slipping. He had seen how firmly the upended rock held the front wheels.

"Truck number fifteen," he whispered to himself.

BRONZE FEATHER
MAKES CONTACT

Bill and Les were looking at the wrecked convertible when Bronze Feather stole back to the truck, keeping well in the shadows. Now he was at the sagging door, now he had a foot up, testing the step. Then he was in the cab, leaning forward from the edge of the seat. A bar of moonlight fell across the wide panel. The switch was—yes, he had it. Now for the earphone. He clicked both switches, but when the crackling sound came, his breath seemed to leave him.

"Truck number fifteen," he croaked.

"Number what?" bawled a voice from the panel.

"Fifteen!" shouted Bronze Feather.

"Where are you?"

But now the men came running from the road, shouting in anger.

"Get out! Want to kill yourself? Get out! Get out!"

The voice in the panel was shouting too. "Where are you? Can't you talk?"

Bronze Feather drew a deep breath. "Near Small Canyon—on the road to Landers—accident —come right away!" he yelled.

Seeing that the truck stood solidly, the men looked up at him with tense faces. "Tell him thirty miles west of Cross-Bar Ranch. Tell him, send big wrecker." Les spoke clearly and distinctly.

Bronze Feather repeated the message.

"Anyone hurt?" came the voice.

"Not bad hurt. But send a doctor!"

"O.K. Who is reporting?"

"Bronze Feather," said the boy proudly.

"No. Your name!" The voice was impatient again.

"Oh, I forgot—I mean John Red Crane," replied Bronze Feather, furious at having made this mistake.

"Tell him, Bill Holand and Les Banks," called Bill. "And then come on down," he added nervously.

When Bronze Feather had repeated the names, the voice said: "O.K., be there in an hour if we can."

Back on the ground, the boy felt light-headed, as if he were a leaf floating in the moonlight. The truck and even the two men seemed unreal. But when Les offered him a cigarette, he saw that the big hand trembled.

"No, thanks, I don't smoke," he said, smiling.

Bill and Les lighted cigarettes, and then Bill held out his left hand. "I'm Bill Holand. I want to thank you. You took an awful chance. I guess you know that."

"Same here," said Les. "We're proud to know you. Arapahoe tribe?"

Bronze Feather nodded, and made haste to ex-

and spoons and tin cups. Little Bud poured the hot coffee.

"Here's to the Red Crane family," said Bill, holding his cup aloft. "Bronze Feather and—and——"

"Little Bud," said her brother. "We're twins. Her English name is Mary."

"We—ell, twins! I thought you looked alike—like peas in a pod. Tell her what you did, how you got us out of this fix."

Bronze Feather backed away. "I can't tell it," he mumbled.

The men gave the account with gusto. They laughed and joked, and the time passed quickly. According to Bill, the hot coffee had even cured the pain in his arm. Every scrap of food was gone and the tin pail was empty when they saw headlights creeping along the highway to the west.

"Before we go—whose wreck of a car was that we hit?" asked Les.

Bronze Feather looked at the ground, pushing a pebble with his foot. "Our father traded our pinto

plain his two names. "Red Crane is my tribe fan
name, and Bronze Feather is my Indian name
has a special meaning—many Indians have s
names. My English name is John; it has no m
ing."

"You know, I never thought of that," said
"Bronze Feather—that's really a nice name,
more interesting than John, or Leslie, or Bil

"William," said Bill, grinning, "if you're ¿
to be formal. But I agree. Indian names are
nicer than our ordinary names."

Were they serious, or were they teasing? B
Feather wasn't sure—but anyway, it didn't
ter, nothing mattered now. . . .

He saw Little Bud coming down the wago
and ran to meet her. She was carrying a
and a covered tin pail.

"You are very happy," she said.

"Oh, yes, I will tell you later," repli
brother, taking the basket.

The meal was spread out on the top o
rock—bread and cheese, a bottle of milk

for it. Then the man he traded with came back and took the wheels off. . . ."

"And the lights and the seats and everything," added Little Bud.

Les gave a whistle. "Some deal. Did he leave it in the road?"

"No. It was off the road."

"Slid down in the rainstorm, I guess," said Bill.

The huge wrecking truck ground slowly up a long grade. A sedan followed. In an hour Bill's arm had been cared for by a doctor and Number 15 was being towed away. Les came up to the twins, who were standing beside the remains of the convertible. "This isn't much. We sure wish we could give you what you deserve." He held out a ten-dollar bill.

Bronze Feather and Little Bud stood as tall and straight as young pines. "Thank you, we don't want any money," said Bronze Feather with dignity. He hesitated and then added, "But if nobody wants the hay and oats, can we have it?"

Les laughed. "Sure thing, and welcome. Our

boss wouldn't fool with it. Would take all summer to get it up!"

Bronze Feather grinned. "We'll get it up. Gee, thank you!"

Little Bud smiled and nodded in agreement. They turned and went quickly up the wagon trail.

When Storm heard their footsteps she raised her head. Her sturdy body cast a shadow over the colt sprawled at her feet. All was silent, silvered— bathed in moonlight. The mare nickered softly as they tiptoed away.

THE LONG HAUL

Bronze Feather made his first trip to the bottom of the chasm at daybreak the next morning. It was no adventure, for he had been there before while hunting. The way down was long and winding, but not steep by the way he took, going down from the wagon trail.

"Ten tons—ten tons," he kept muttering as he hurried along, and tried to imagine how much hay and oats that would be, and where he would store it all, and how long it would take to get it up. The mare? No, he could not take the time to train her, and the evil pinto had——

He rounded a turn. The treasure was just

below, spread out before him. Heaped—piled—
tossed, hurled out over ledges and spilling down
the sides of gigantic boulders. Golden oats, pale
green hay—it dripped from crevices and rocky
setbacks. There was no end to it; it seemed to
cover the earth!

In the midst of it stood the pinto, too busy to do
more than raise his head briefly at Bronze Feather's
approach. The poor animal still wore his bridle,
the broken reins hanging from the bit. Scrawny,
hammer-headed, but still very much alive.

Bronze Feather stopped. This was too much—
he was surely waking from a dream, for the prob-
lem of getting all this up was now solved. The
pinto could be captured. The trick was to show
no interest in him, but little by little move closer
until he could be caught by the bridle reins. The
device always worked. It worked now. In fact,
the pinto seemed glad of human company and nickered at the boy's approach. He even tolerated some
stroking and stood quiet while an armful of hay
and a bag of oats were loaded on his swayed back.

154

"Come along now; we are going home," said Bronze Feather.

Up and up they went, to the wagon trail and then on to the cabin. Little Bud was making breakfast and, hearing the clink of hoofs, she ran to the door. She began to laugh, and laughed until tears ran down her cheeks. The pinto standing at the steps turned his head to look at her in wonder.

"Touch him! He is real!" cried Bronze Feather, and, throwing the reins to her, he leaped and cavorted around the yard. Sobered at last, he explained what had happened, a thing almost too strange to believe.

"The hay and oats have come down from the cliff like a waterfall. Even with the pinto we can never get it all up," he ended in a worried voice.

Later they took the hay and a pail of oats down to the corral, where it was first sniffed at and then nibbled by Wildwing and the mare. But because they were wild horses, oats and hay were new to them. They were looking for their usual morning feeding of carrots and green corn.

"They will eat it when they are really hungry," Bronze Feather said.

The pinto was harnessed and hitched to the wagon. The twins worked all day, taking the whole bags of oats and the unbroken bales of hay first. The pinto was patient about the long climb up to the trail where they had left the wagon, and even allowed Little Bud to pull the burs from his mane while they were resting between trips. By sunset a large pile was stored under the pines near the cabin.

But riches bring worries. When a few scattered clouds appeared over the mountains Bronze Feather watched them with a sober face. Clouds might mean rain, and rain would spoil the oats. He went down to the corral. At sight of him, Wildwing and Storm left the pile of hay and came hurrying over to the bars.

"Ah ha, you did not want me to catch you eating the hay," he said, swinging up to sit on the top rail. The colt nudged and bunted with his head, plainly asking for something besides caresses. The boy's hand slipped from Wildwing to touch the mare. He stroked the coarse mane, straightening and smoothing the tangled strands. She stood quiet, accepting the attention, and even snapped at the young one when he came pushing between them. Now would be the time to begin her training, he thought, to put a rope on her and teach her to lead. He sighed and jumped down from the bars. That would have to wait.

He examined the sky before going to bed that night. It was safely star-spangled, but in his dreams he was wading waist deep in oats, holding out his sombrero to protect them from a storm. The clouds rolled overhead, but instead of rain, loose hay began to sprinkle down.

"Tons and tons," he mumbled, and woke up.

Sunlight streamed in through the windows. Still his dream was so vivid that he could hardly believe it wasn't raining. He dressed quickly and went out. Little Bud was gathering firewood. She had been up for hours. The cow was milked and all the chores were done.

"Come, I will show you something!" she cried,

157

and ran toward the meadow. Her brother followed, his eyes still blinking with sleep.

At the top of a knoll they stopped. *Two* horses were grazing side by side, one solid black, the other black and white. Storm and the pinto.

"They are friends now," Little Bud said, beaming. "And she has not been in the cornfield. I looked and there were no tracks."

"Are you sure?"

"I am sure. She came to join the pinto because she was lonely. She misses her wild companions, I think."

The horses raised their heads and stood watching as Bronze Feather and Little Bud came slowly toward them. The pinto, being haltered and hobbled, would be easy to catch. Still, he could be ugly if he had a mind to bite. But now he came bobbing forward as if anxious to show his new friend that *he* had no fear of humans. Storm followed and, coming up beside the pinto, snapped at him when he seemed to be getting more attention than she was.

158

"Look—look, she's putting her nose in my hand!" exclaimed Little Bud.

Bronze Feather slipped the hobbles from the pinto's legs and straightened up. "That's because she thinks you're a carrot," he said soberly.

They went through the meadow and clattered down the trail to the spring. Wildwing whinnied from the corral. Storm answered and, trotting ahead, made her usual neat flight over the bars.

An hour later the pinto was tied to a sapling at the bottom of the chasm. A pile of loose hay lay in front of him, but his eyes were on the rivers of grain heap and flowing among the rock crevices.

"There is so much—we could not gather it in a whole summer," sighed Little Bud. She was scooping the oats up with a tin pan and pouring them into a half-filled bag. The few bags that had not broken open in the fall down the cliff had already been stored under the pines near the cabin. Now the twins were gathering the others that were torn beyond use. Sometimes loose grain showered down from the cliffs above, where empty

bags, caught on the rocks, flapped in the wind like washing on a line.

When Bronze Feather had tied the tops of two bags with string he heaved them up on the pinto's back. "There is not much time," he worried. "We must also build a shed. If it rains, we will lose much of the oats."

They worked all morning under a blazing sun, and when eight bags had been taken up and piled in the wagon, Bronze Feather led the pinto down for the midday rest and feeding. Little Bud had brought their own lunch in a basket. They ate in the shade beside a small stream and then lay on the rocks, watching the crows and magpies that had come to share in the feast of grain. Squirrels and chipmunks made tiny rustlings and scurryings; the whole chasm was alive with small bright-eyed creatures.

Suddenly Bronze Feather sat up. The motor they had been hearing on the highway above had come to a stop, and a tiny figure had appeared at the rim of the great wall. Two others joined it.

161

"Look," the boy whispered. "Some people are watching us."

The twins stared upward. Maybe someone had come to get the hay and grain after all. Maybe even the bags and bales they had taken would have to be given back! Now one of the figures was pointing, perhaps at the pinto, which was standing in full sight. Maybe they had field glasses and could see clearly even at this distance.

"One looks like a woman," whispered Little Bud. The clear liquid call of a whippoorwill came. A whippoorwill in the middle of the day? The call came again—a pause, and then three in quick succession. They knew *that* signal.

"Our grandfather!" they shouted, and ran out, waving their arms.

The meeting was a joyous one, with questions and answers flying back and forth. When the pinto had been harnessed and hitched to the wagon, Bronze Feather said, "You have had a long walk, Grandfather. There is room on the wagon for you to ride."

162

"We have not walked," Gray Wolf said quickly. "I have a fine car back at the highway. When your mother and grandfather came to the garage this morning I had much to tell," he added proudly.

The boy looked at his mother, but now she was smiling. "It is so. Many things have happened," she said. "Your father learned of the accident only yesterday, when a man came to see him at the garage."

"And this man handed me forty dollars," exclaimed Gray Wolf.

"Forty dollars! What for?" cried Bronze Feather, thinking that his father had accepted payment for what *they* had done to help the truck drivers.

Gray Wolf held up his hand for silence. "For having with great foresight traded our pinto for a car. That car was struck by a truck, as you know. That was against the law, also it damaged the car. To pay for the damage, the insurance company paid me forty dollars. That money I put on a payment for another car."

"But the old one had no wheels—" began Bronze Feather in bewilderment.

Gray Wolf drew himself up. This was his greatest triumph.

"Because of my knowledge of the ways of the white man I have brought us great riches: hundreds of dollars' worth of hay and oats, and another car! Also, we have the pinto," he added.

Little Bud wanted to giggle, but, meeting her brother's warning glance, she sobered. There was nothing to say, no way of understanding their father. Bronze Feather led the pinto ahead and they walked along in silence.

Now Gray Wolf, who had been speaking in Arapahoe out of respect for the grandfather, broke into English. "The new car runs like a bobcat! It's a Packard sedan, 1935. They really made cars in those days. All it needs is a few new parts."

The grandfather, Long Bow, had not spoken, but now and then a faint smile came over the old wrinkled face. Despite his eighty years, his stride was strong and firm as he walked beside his grandson. "Running Water has told me of the foal. How is it with him?"

Bronze Feather's face lit up. "Wildwing is back. He is now in the corral with——" He stopped, staring ahead.

Storm was standing under a tree. The colt was nursing beside her, his wispy tail flicking back and forth.

THE OLD CHIEF

Wildwing blew at the oats and then, quickly re-capturing the lively grains, munched them with a steady grinding of his supple jaws. Next to his plump roundness the mare looked clumsy. But even she was filling out; her coat was smoother and she had lost most of her wild frightened look.

Bronze Feather and the grandfather leaned on the corral bars. They had led the colt back and Storm had followed. "She must have kicked the bars down when she jumped," the boy said. "I cannot build anything well, it seems. I have not learned that yet."

Long Bow turned to look at his grandson. "You

have done well. In days past any chief would have been proud to ride such a horse as you have captured and tamed."

"But he is only a foal," the boy said humbly.

"That is best. Taken as a foal, he will learn to know you and trust you. Also, you will learn to know and trust him. You will grow up together and have love for each other. My first horse was such a one. But black—black and shining, like a raven's wing."

"Tell me about him," the boy said eagerly.

"Oh, I have told you many times." The old chief's black eyes looked off toward the mountains. "I named him Raven, for he flew like a bird, but he would also come at my signal. We had love for each other, but that was a long time past. . . ."

Long Bow fell silent. The boy waited, for he knew that his grandfather's thoughts were not here, but in a time remembered. He himself would never know such glories as were in Long Bow's memory, but neither did he share his grandfather's deep resentment of the white man. To hold such bitterness was a bad thing, his mother had taught him. Still, he loved his grandfather deeply, and wished that he would stay with them always, instead of coming for visits.

"There were great chiefs in days past. Men who were fearless and who did what they believed was right. You also would have grown up to be one, I think." Long Bow spoke sadly.

"I can still be a chief, Grandfather," replied the boy. "A new kind of chief."

"Now you speak like your father, Gray Wolf. He thinks only of the new. Real wisdom lies in knowledge of the old."

"I know that, Grandfather, for you have taught me. But our mother says that we must also have knowledge of the new. If I continue in school, I may someday be a teacher or a writer. Then I will be able to tell about our people, the Arapahoe, and how we have learned both the old ways and the new."

Long Bow looked at the boy's ardent young face. "That is true. And you have spoken well. For a great chief has wisdom and also kindness.

Perhaps even white men will learn something from you in time to come."

Wildwing had come up to the bars and stood for a moment, watching them. Then, as if impatient at their lack of attention, he rose straight up on his hind legs and pawed the air. He pranced and wheeled this way and that, bouncing up and down as if he were on springs. Then off around the corral with head flung back, tail erect, his hoofs barely touching the ground.

His wild spirits were contagious; the mare threw up her head and galloped with him, showing the uncanny skill of her wild kind in the placing of their feet. For in this small space she wheeled and turned with almost no loss of speed, and Long Bow, watching, saw again what he had seen in his youth—the great plains, and the great herds of riderless horses.

"See how she turns—she is beautiful," the boy said under his breath.

His grandfather nodded. "All horses are beautiful to those who love them."

"Will you help me with her training?" Bronze

Feather asked eagerly. "She is not wild any more. You saw how she followed us, and she lets me stroke her mane."

"Then we will begin now. She is used to your scent. Put your scarf around her neck and lead her around the corral," said Long Bow.

Bronze Feather slid over the bars, and when Storm and the colt came up he was waiting with his large red cowboy handkerchief in his hand. He stroked them both, and then let Storm smell the handkerchief. Then slowly and very gently he slipped it around her neck and tied the ends in a loose knot. She stood quietly.

"Now lead her, but do not pull if she does not wish to go," directed Long Bow. "And also speak to her," he added.

That part was easy; the boy had been sharing his thoughts with colt and mare all summer. "Now you are learning," he began, "the same as I learn at school. Only this is easier—it is not like spelling or arithmetic." As he spoke he moved a step, pulling gently at the handkerchief.

Storm had been listening with eyes half closed. Now she followed. They plodded slowly around the corral with the colt tagging behind. Round and round they went, first in one direction and then the other. The mare made the turns as patiently as an old plow horse. On the last turn, Long Bow took down the bars and signaled to them to pass on out of the corral.

They went up the trail, stopping at the spring for a drink, and then along toward the cabin. Bronze Feather felt as if he were floating on a cloud. *Storm was tamed! She was following his guidance—not going her own way.* He had actually tamed a wild horse!

"It goes well," said Long Bow. "Now we must try the halter."

The pinto, still harnessed and tied to a tree, nickered at their approach. The boy led Storm to the tree where the pinto's halter hung from a branch. He took it down and let her smell it.

Long Bow brought some oats in his sombrero. The halter was slipped over Storm's nose and the oats were quickly offered. After that came more leading and much flattery from the elated Bronze Feather. The lesson ended with a blanket and then half a bag of oats being placed gently on her back. Long Bow led the mare back to the corral. The boy followed with an armful of hay.

In a few days Storm was helping the pinto carry hay and oats up from the chasm. Sometimes the colt tagged along, wearing the tiny rawhide halter Bronze Feather made for him.

A new shed to house the hay and grain rose slowly under the pines. Even Gray Wolf was interested in this project and often drove out after work, bringing building supplies and even bags to hold the loose grain. He was doing well at his job in the garage, and with a car to drive he seemed more content, and certainly more energetic.

"Now we're in business," he said, clapping his hand over Bronze Feather's shoulder. "Got a rancher coming out with his truck. He'll take all the hay and oats we can get out to the highway. Pay top price too. Feed's scarce this year."

"We will not sell what is in the shed. That belongs to the boy and to the three horses," replied Running Water quietly. "If there is more than we need for this winter and for the next summer, we can sell that."

But for once Gray Wolf was right. There was much to sell and much left over. It turned out to be a good year for the Red Crane family. The corn and the garden prospered, they had a good team of horses and a new shed. The hay and the grain had been a gift from the Great Spirit Above, and though there had been much labor in bringing it up, they were very thankful. This and much more Long Bow spoke of one evening when they were gathered around the fireplace in the cabin.

They were to leave in the morning. All was packed and ready, everyone anxious to go. Running Water got up and went to the door. She had been watching for Gray Wolf's lantern to come along the wagon trail, but now she saw two bright headlights in the far distance and heard the grind of a laboring motor.

174

Then they all heard it and ran out. The car pulled into the yard and made a neat turn. Gray Wolf stepped out. "I made it!" he called. "I knew she could do it—road just needs a little fixing, that's all."

And so it was that the mother left the cabin in the style that Gray Wolf thought was proper— riding in a car, not a wagon. But until they reached the highway, where the car picked up speed, Running Water often turned to watch the wagon, which was following slowly behind. Long Bow, who had spurned the car, was driving. Little Bud minded the cow, which was tethered to the back of the wagon, and Bronze Feather led Wildwing by a rawhide rein.

"This new one goes well in harness," said Long Bow. "But she will not let the spotted one lead— she must always be ahead."

But the boy did not hear. He was racing ahead with Wildwing.

Bronze Feather found the bulky envelope on

the kitchen table when he and Little Bud came home from school. He picked it up and turned it over. "Frederick A. Rand. Who could that be?" he puzzled.

"And look how it's addressed! Mr. Feather and Miss Little Bud! Not even our last name. How did it ever get to us?" exclaimed his sister. A letter addressed to them, especially an airmail letter, was so unusual that at first she wondered if they should open it before their mother came home.

"But it is for us," said Bronze Feather, and opened the envelope, being careful not to tear into the return address.

A sheaf of colored snapshots spilled out on the table. "It's from Fred—the man who took our pictures last summer!" he yelped. "I forgot all about him!"

Little Bud spread the snapshots out. "They're beautiful," she murmured, "just beautiful."

There was one of Bronze Feather on horseback, and one of him stepping out of the cabin. A sad one of a tan and white colt half buried in sand,

and one from the rock rim where the horses had fallen. The rest were of Little Bud, some sober, some smiling. They went over them one by one, and suddenly Little Bud shrieked with laughter. "Look—look at this one of me. That little white spot! That's Wildwing's nose!"

"Where? Let me see!"

"Here, at the edge of the big skirt!"

Bronze Feather examined the picture. "I guess it is. Must be. But it looks like a ball of white yarn or something."

"Oh, no, it's Wildwing. I was using dark blue yarn. There's a note in the envelope. Read it— maybe he says something about it," said Little Bud.

But the note said only: "Hope you like these, and thanks for a wonderful day, and for teaching me some things I didn't know before. Hope to be out again next summer. Best wishes, Fred."

Little Bud rolled her eyes in a gesture of relief. "He didn't see Wildwing—that was just luck!"

"Mmm," mumbled her brother. He was reading the note again. ". . . *and for teaching me some-*

thing I didn't know before." What did that mean? How had they taught this man anything? Maybe he meant about the wild horses and why they were hunted with planes. Yes, that must be it, he thought, and put the note back in the envelope.

"Now I wish he had seen Wildwing. Then we'd have whole pictures of him—not just the tip of his nose," said Little Bud.

Bronze Feather didn't answer for a while. He was still thinking about the note and what that sentence had meant. "I think we should tell him when we write to him," he said at last.

"Tell him what?" asked Little Bud.

"About the colt—and why we hid him, and about the other horses. He says that we taught him something he did not know before. I think he has also taught *us* something. That we should not be suspicious of people, that we should try to understand them. . . ."

Little Bud wanted to smile, but her brother was serious, she knew, for he spoke in their own language. "You speak like our mother and like our

178

teachers," she said in Arapahoe. "But I think you are right. We should tell him. For he has faith in us, and believes as we do in many things. We should have faith in him too. We will write the letter together."

The letter was not easy to write. The whole Red Crane family worked at it. The reply came by telegram; just one line.

CANT WAIT TO PHOTOGRAPH WILDWING IN COLOR

There was a smell of autumn on the wind. The harvest moon, waxed and yellowed according to the season, hung nightly over the silent cabin, the newly built shed, and the somber pines. In the daytime, goldenrod and asters spread their varied colors for the sun's warm light. But high on the ridges a blanket of snow had sifted down. In time it would cover Wildwing's small oval hoofprints, and the larger, deeper prints left by Storm and the pinto, and the long ribbon of wagon track that led out to the highway.

Snow and sleet would cover and soften the cliffs that hung over the grotto, and over the high-lifted wall above the chasm. But under the snow, water would still move. Hoofs would stamp through it, hoofs that dug for mosses and grass and lichen would sometimes find hay, or a pocket of moisture-swelled oats. Sometimes the spaces would ring with a wild call, the call of the buckskin stallion.